Praise for *The Corruption of Zachary R.*

In staccato chapters dealt out like a deck of cards—
snappy, latent, repeating—Richardson tracks Zachary
R.'s descent into psychosis. It is not a combustible
event, but rather quotidian, and its very everydayness
makes it especially creepy and troubling. Richardson
explores the faults and folds of Zachary's life—his
father's obsession with chess, his mother's comic-but-
for-its-ramifications death, the concussive darkness of
his marriage, his daughter's colorful waywardness—in
writing that has the elemental quality and dreamy,
out-of-body remoteness of black-and-white
photography. . . . Repetition is a powerful leitmotif in
the author's arsenal . . . and he deploys it with a
Hitchcockian fatality. . . . Diverting customers appear
and reappear to usher Zachary toward his rewards,
talismanic elements hit the reader like doomful claps
of thunder—brass knuckles, chess pieces, rivers and
women. Richardson tenders characters that, due to
the story's brevity and swiftness, are quickly
sympathetic and pack a compressed punch. . . . An
artful, beguiling voyage.

-Kirkus Discoveries

There is a certain yin and yang to Richardson's work
that moves us to quickly invest ourselves in his
characters. The novel sails along in short bursts of
revelations. . . . [Richardson] writes with a poet's
heart and a suspense novelist's eye.

-ForeWord Reviews

Also by Douglas Richardson

Ghosts in Time and Space
2011

Poems for Loners
2010

Out in the Cold, Cold Day
2009

Sugar Fish
2007

The Corruption of Zachary R.

Douglas Richardson

Weak Creature Press
Los Angeles

The Corruption of Zachary R.
© 2009 by Douglas Richardson
Weak Creature Press
First Printing, October 2009

Library of Congress Control Number: 2009936564
ISBN: 978-0-9842424-1-2

Printed in the United States of America.

Cover design by Heather DeSerio, Precision Edge Design LLC.

Author photo by Reggie Ige, Your Moment Forever Photography.

For information on other publications available from Weak Creature Press, please email weakcreature@aol.com.

Contents

For Michele

PART I

1. Committed

The bun held the burger. The wrapper held the bun. The brown bag held the whole apparatus, concealing what was happening to the burger: worms, microbes, malodor.

Zachary R. was committed on a thin autumn Saturday, Nebraska football on a New England lawn, a dad mowing at halftime, vibrations on his right-angle chin.

His teenage daughter, keeper of the ash, put on the Revolution Dress and went to the blood drive on an empty stomach. She returned home like scurvy over anemia, crashing the Nova through the living room window. He kissed her and sent her to her room with a grapefruit and a Hershey's, and he set about surrounding the house with orange cones to distract the eyes of the neighbors.

The burger had festered for days in the abandoned shed on the riverbank and Zachary R. wanted to care for it, so he set off on foot saying,

3

"Service to mankind, Service to mankind." For eight miles, however, he went tenement to tenement eating numbers right off the doors, stealing the identities of tenants to the delight of landlords and Goth Girls, who clutched their Damien lockets and swooned at the sight of the rusty nails in his lips and the brown blood hugging his neck.

A month later, in the asylum, he claimed to the Cracked Snail, "I have Neosporin." Only the snail heard him.

A year later, someone important heard him say, "I like rivers and women." These words got him permission to mow the asylum lawn, vibrations on his right-angle chin saying, "Service to mankind, Service to mankind."

2. Seven Women Walking in Lab Coats

Zachary R. sat in the exact middle of the asylum lawn on a chair that made a pattern on his legs.

He was daydreaming about pine trees and leisure until he looked through the iron bars of the gate and saw seven women walking in lab coats, cameras raised to cover their spying faces. These women were posing as health care journalists. Their badges indicated that they were doing a photo exposé for *Psychiatry Today*, but their black painted eyes and lips and fingernails indicated otherwise.

Zachary R. looked down at the Cracked Snail and asked, "How do I bed one?"

The snail replied, "Approach the redhead.

"Tell her she's somewhat gorgeous, that chess is nearly impossible.

"Tell her you need to look far away to erase her naked image from your mind."

Zachary R. heard the sound of a plane. He looked at the sky.

3. Chess

Bishop takes knight. Pawn takes bishop. Pawn takes queen.

Zachary R. lay in bed in the asylum, tense as a gargoyle, unbearably awake because of chess with his father.

The lessons soldered his cerebrum. His cerebrum short-circuited: Leave the knights on the back row. Be aggressive with the rooks. Move the queen out as quickly as possible.

So many hypotheticals. So much losing.

And the board itself, each square a minor concussion.

Insomnia troubled him until dawn, when at last he slept for an hour, then awoke erect as a saint with no one to touch.

Sometimes it calmed him to picture Earth from space:

The blue and white eye.

The slow reentry.

Mother with child in subway.

4. Keeper of the Ash

Solitary, poor, nasty, brutish, and short.

Zachary R.'s teenage daughter, a Hobbes scholar with a nose ring, understood how in one moment a bag lady could look down at the veins in her thighs and in the next moment be the victim in a fatal hit and run.

Sarah R. was her name and she was filled with pity, which is four-fifths of piety, which is an obsession with the sanctity of death, which meant her father had obligated her to guard the urn with her mother's ashes.

Sarah R. arrived in New Orleans in early February, on the Wednesday before Mardi Gras. She checked into a bargain motel, unpacked, threw on the Revolution Dress, drank all the liquor in the minibar, shaved her head, and went to the corner for a hot dog. She watched mustard and onions splatter on the sidewalk, disrupting a trail of ants. She felt omnipotent like Hobbes' Leviathan, until she stumbled into the street and was nearly struck by a speeding bus. The hot dog vendor picked her up and escorted her back to her room. He kissed her on the cheek and slipped his business card in her cleavage.

5. The Dungeon

Sarah R. woke Thursday afternoon in Necropolis, in New Orleans, the estuary, city of brackish voodoo, turtle soup, and hurricanes.

It was true. The hot dog vendor had slipped his business card in her cleavage the night before, only it wasn't a business card for his hot dog cart. Rather, it read of his capacity as bartender and part owner of the Dungeon, a bar in the French Quarter.

The Dungeon was situated at the end of a long, narrow alley. Its hours were from midnight to an undisclosed hour just after sunrise.

Sarah R. slipped into the Revolution Dress and arrived at the Dungeon after midnight on Friday morning, sans urn, on an empty stomach.

She was there for more self-destruction.

Blue Hawaiians and blow jobs were the drinks of the night.

There were mannequin menageries and foul rubber masques. T-shirts were being sold.

She danced with a grateful deadhead who said as if in a dream, "You are adroit."

She looked up that word after she woke Friday afternoon.

6. The Same Sensation as a Feather Boa

All Saturday afternoon and into Saturday evening, Sarah R. wandered the streets of the French Quarter in a vain attempt to find the deadhead from the night before. In addition to the word *adroit*, she recalled him saying something about returning to Kentucky and the word *Godspeed*.

She stopped at Café Du Monde for chicory coffee. The hot dog vendor wheeled his cart along the sidewalk, but he did not stop to chat with her. Instead, he winked an avuncular wink and moved through the cold February night.

Sarah R. returned to her room and lay in bed, but she did not sleep.

Sunday morning she put on the Revolution Dress, ate eggs Benedict that made her eyes throb, and took the urn in a cab to Lake Pontchartrain, where she paid a fee and boarded a tour boat.

About a mile offshore, Sarah R. maneuvered her way to the bow and, in a moment of sheer adolescent impetuousness, emptied the contents of the urn into the brackish water.

The captain of the vessel, who had watched Sarah from the start (it wasn't every day he saw young women board his tour boat with urns under their arms), was bound by law to inform her that the disposal of human ashes had to be formally cleared by the Neptune Society. Sarah R. replied, "When some of the ashes blew back into my face, it was the same sensation as a feather boa."

The captain was sufficiently bewitched by this response to invite her for turtle soup and mint juleps after the boat had docked.

She declined the invitation. Relieved, he removed the handkerchief from his shirt pocket, wiped the residue from her face, and made an awkward remark about how the Neptune Society would be outraged if they ever found out.

Sarah R. returned to the city, swinging the empty urn low as a pendulum, waxing reverent as stained glass at dawn.

7. The Revolution Dress

Stardust in her backpack, flask in her pocket, opium in her veins. But nothing intoxicated Sarah R. more than the Revolution Dress.

It made her burn with weakness.

It made her reckless and charitable.

It was blood drives and blackjack, kittens and heroin.

It was apples and arsenic and trick-or-treating with foster parents.

When the hot dog vendor was asked to describe Sarah R., he said, "Her charm was like a shade of burgundy I hadn't noticed before."

Of course he wasn't describing Sarah R., but the Revolution Dress.

The Revolution Dress was five times eight, eight times thirteen, thirteen times twenty-one, twenty-one times thirty-four, and so on, but then it was all divided by zero.

8. Antipsychotic Oblivion

Droperidol. Haloperidol. Lorazepam. Diazepam.

Believing his discharge from the asylum was imminent, Zachary R. complied with his regimen. The antipsychotics had the following side effects:

Sheep and clouds.

Sky and grass.

Sand and water.

Fire and ash.

He imagined that Sarah handed him the urn. He opened it and stared at the ashes, searching for humanity. He closed the urn and looked out the asylum window. Again he imagined Sarah.

"Can you forgive me?" he asked.

9. Antipsychotic Hallucination

The medication moved through his body like panic moves through a crowd, every nerve scraped and startled, every memory ambiguous and addled.

He entered a forest where boxcars stretched endlessly through tunnels in hills with shacks and cigarettes.

The Cold Angel ran her veil over his scalp. Fog passed above and diagonally. "They're there for you to ride," she said. "Why won't you play in them?"

The Cold Angel joined at his side, rubbed his back like winter, and asked "Whatever happened to the child in you?"

He wept, but not over his lost childhood. He wept because of what the boxcars had done.

"Lie down under a picnic table and sleep," she said, "and the train will go away."

10. Memories of the Carnival

The best day of Zachary R.'s life was the day his daughter was born. The second-best day of Zachary R.'s life was the day his daughter was conceived, which was at the carnival. Therefore, Zachary R. liked the carnival. He made a bullet-point list of his memories of the carnival on that day:

- Hay bales
- Ropes

- Logs

- Parachutes

- Flashing colors

- Historical photos

- Brown

- Earth

- Smoke

- Among strangers

- Rolls of tickets

- Stolen

- Torn

- Dropped into a slot in a metal box

11. Flyswatter by the Toilet

In the days and nights leading up to his committal, Zachary R. kept a flyswatter by the toilet for use as an emetic. Each time before he got sick, he swung the flyswatter while reciting these words:

Forehand

Backhand

Microphone

Guitar

Spider on shoulder

Cockroach on soap bar

Slipping

Slipping

Slipping

12. The Last Night at the House

Toilet was sterilized. Flyswatter was packed. Fridge was warm and empty. Asylum was in the past.

Zachary R. had just closed the door of his house for the last time when it occurred to him that the walls needed sponging with mild dish soap.

He turned the doorknob, but the door was locked and the key was in a business reply envelope on its way to *Playboy* magazine.

He considered the definition of insanity: "to do the same thing over and over and expect different results." He went to the bar anyway.

Zachary R. spoke to no one there, except for the bartender the seven times he ordered drinks. The bar was crowded with the din of human voices, but sometimes single voices could be heard saying things like:

"Cigar boxes and romance novels are the brass knuckles of sex."

Or, "I am nostalgic for the dark-road signature of the skunk."

Or, "Are you lonely as the cello? No, I am lonely as an aisle of concrete in the moonlight."

When he realized it was he who had uttered these things, Zachary R. knew he should leave.

He exited out the back, stinking of bourbon but feeling better about his chances of entering his ex-home.

He picked up several substantial stones on the way, expecting he would need to bust a window to get inside. To his moderate surprise, however, the door was unlocked when he arrived. He went room to room looking for signs of an intruder, but found none. Perplexed, and more than a little drunk, he entered the kitchen and opened the cupboard that held the cleaning supplies. He took a sponge and some dish soap and began sponging.

He sponged the dining room and the study, the hallways and the bedrooms, all without incident. But when he arrived in the living room, his attention was diverted by several ants and a termite on the windowsill.

He watched the ants surround the termite and the ensuing carnage: Six ants amputated six termite legs, two ants amputated two termite wings, and a ninth ant arrived to carry off the termite body.

Zachary R. paused and then proclaimed, "International harvesters."

Then he thought, "What is this merciless carnival I am allowing in my home?"

He emptied the entire bottle of soap onto the victorious ants and sponged the whole ensemble.

He reached into his pockets and grabbed the substantial stones. He knocked out the boards where the living room window had been, and he ripped and tore the carpet on the living room floor. He busted out the remaining windows and pounded divots into the walls.

He busted and pounded until the vicious energy was gone. Then, exhausted, he went outside and sat on a stack of pine logs that he had cut with a sharp axe. He thought about the dead and wondered where he was in the years before his birth. He smiled the eyeless smile of eradicated dreams.

PART II

13. Bernrd Red

Countless boys came into existence the same year as Zachary R., but none had as much influence on his fate as one of the many boys who were called Bernard. Because the father of this Bernard, for various reasons, refused to lend the boy his last name, this Bernard adopted the street name of his mother, the roughhouse prostitute. His mother's street name was Chloe Red.

And one day, for various reasons, Bernard Red decided to remove the "a" from his name to promote the sensation of being hit in the head with a rock.

There are many rumors surrounding Bernrd Red, all of which have been substantiated. One such rumor was that Bernrd Red was a pious child until he got hit in the face by a girl.

14. The Roughhouse Prostitute

Bernrd Red was a pious child until he got hit in the face by a girl; and by girl, it was the girl he referred to as "Mother," which is to say, his mother had him when she was fifteen years old.

Bernrd Red's father was one H. Charles Branhoover, a well-to-do and good-for-nothing banker in the city all three lived in: Pittsburgh, Pennsylvania.

All three lived in Pittsburgh, but not under one roof. Branhoover didn't want the scandal that would surely have arisen from a fifty-one-year-old man living with his fifteen-year-old lover and their baby. So he set lover and child up in a one-bedroom apartment, and he hired a crew of good-natured but aggressive nannies, who delivered money and groceries and ensured that the boy, whom mother and father named Bernard, received an education fit for a Branhoover, even if the child couldn't take the Branhoover name.

The nannies taught Bernard to read and write, and up to Algebra-level mathematics, all while immersed in Mozart and the music of the sixties and seventies. And all this was accomplished by the time Bernard turned eight, when he was enrolled in the Pittsburgh public school system.

Chloe Red loved her boy, but she knew life wasn't all Mozart, Crosby, Stills, Nash & Young, and mathematical precociousness. There was also the knowledge she possessed, street knowledge. Chloe Red resented the bossy nannies and the money and her secret life, so she resolved that her contribution to her son's upbringing would be to instill a little of the hard reality of the streets, which is to say she taught him how to fight and how not to be a sissy.

Bernard, of course, preferred his time with the nannies and the music and his studies over his time with his mother. Of course, his mother didn't like this fact.

The fighting lessons became less like lessons and more like punishments. The blows Chloe administered to Bernard became less and less playful and instructive, and rose from taps to the stomach to blows to the arms and the face. When the blows to the face began, Bernard Red began to change.

15. Bernrd Red, Crosby, Stills, Nash & Young

When he was very young, Bernard Red loved music. His mother's clientele even said of him, "That boy of yours has a real affinity for music." These remarks were made mainly in the family room, where the record player was located. Not only did he love the Mozart foisted on him by aggressive nannies, but also he loved "Puff the Magic Dragon" and "One Little Two Little Three Little Indians." Actually, regarding the latter, he mainly liked it because the record label was tan and red, which he imagined to be the colors of the Indians. Tan and red coated his mind like pink bismuth coated his parents' stomachs.

Bernard Red's favorite band was Crosby, Stills, Nash & Young, even though he told everyone he liked Led Zeppelin best.

He played CSNY at every opportunity until he entered the public school in the third grade and it was discovered that he excelled at math, surpassing even Betsy Sullivan, who was also the class bully.

Betsy Sullivan didn't like it when Bernard Red outdid her on every math exam, so one morning she confronted him at recess. He tried to appease her by inviting her over to listen to Led Zeppelin. Betsy responded by hitting him square in the forehead. Bernard hit her back, but by that time the teachers had descended upon the commotion, witnessing only Bernard's retaliation.

Three days later, after serving his suspension for hitting a girl, Bernard Red sat in the principal's office filling out reinstatement forms when he blurted out, "Betsy Sullivan is a fussy wet salami."

From that day on, Betsy Sullivan regained her favored status among the faculty.

From that day on, Bernard Red dedicated himself to collecting substantial stones for breaking school windows and for bruising student skulls.

From that day on, Bernard Red began omitting the "a" from his name on all of his homework, which one of his more eccentric teachers said gave her the same sensation as being hit in the head with a rock.

16. Preppie Hoodlum

By the time they entered high school, Bernrd Red and Betsy Sullivan had put aside their differences. In fact, the two of them had been an item since middle school, when, as a happy couple, they terrorized their fellow students and each other to their mutual delight and to the chagrin of their teachers.

Bernrd Red would call Betsy Sullivan a fussy wet salami just so they could fight and make up with barbaric sex in the afternoon before Betsy's parents got home (and sometimes at Bernrd's home, but not as often because Chloe Red was usually there with her Johns earning extra money on the sly because her well-to-do and good-for-nothing banker husband was cheap). At night they would sneak out and meet up to gather substantial stones for busting out the windows of the school, which made them whirl and pop and believe they were in love.

By now, Bernrd Red believed in the strength of violence and the weakness of music. He renounced Mozart and Led Zeppelin and he obliterated Crosby, Stills, Nash & Young from his mind.

Betsy said he should try to get into punk rock but Bernrd Red refused, saying punk was for poseurs and pussies seeking attention. So Betsy Sullivan dressed like a punk rocker to antagonize Bernrd Red, and Bernrd Red dressed like a preppie hoodlum to antagonize Betsy Sullivan, and they whirled and popped and busted out the school windows until graduation, when Bernrd Red ended their relationship without explanation.

17. Self-Styled Cooler

Bernrd Red was silently distraught over the end of his relationship with Betsy Sullivan, despite having been the one to call it off. He understood that breaking up with Betsy was a cowardly thing to do, but he did it anyway to maintain his image as a preppie hoodlum.

Although Betsy cried and broke things around the house, her broken heart only took about a week to mend, and then she settled down, went to nursing school, became a nurse and an adult, and never gave her ex another thought.

Bernrd Red, on the other hand, bummed around the streets of Pittsburgh promoting the sensation of being hit in the head with a rock. If there was a street brawl or a bruised skull or a broken window, Bernrd Red was likely to blame.

His father, H. Charles Branhoover, the well-to-do and good-for-nothing banker, tried his best to rein in his wayward son. But when his son threw a rock through the window of Mr.

Branhoover's bank with a note attached that read, "Dear Mr. Branhoover: Hi Dad. Sorry I forgot your birthday whenever it was this past year. Here is your belated birthday present. Don't get mad. Rocks make good paperweights for a busy bank executive's desk. Your son, Bernrd Red-Branhoover," Mr. Branhoover wasted no time getting his son out of town for good.

When Bernrd Red learned that "out of town for good" meant he was being sent away to the School of Hotel Management at the University of Nevada, Las Vegas, he cooperated in every way possible to expedite his expulsion from Pittsburgh.

In Las Vegas, Bernrd Red became an "A" student and a self-styled cooler at the Golden Horseshoe downtown, where he won on the come line and quieted the craps tables with no expectation of reward other than the desire to watch other gamblers lose. He caught the appreciative eyes of the pit bosses and the casino owner, who made Bernrd Red his protégé, which Bernrd took full advantage of.

Bernrd Red and the casino owner rigged the roulette wheel and canoodled with showgirls. Bernrd Red's slogan at the rigged roulette wheel was "Always bet on black," but the rigged roulette wheel was rigged to land on red. Bernrd Red enjoyed watching the various expressions of dismay on the faces of the gamblers when, despite his advice to bet on black, and the gamblers following his advice, he moved his chips to red at the last second, just before the dealer waved his hand over the table signaling no more bets, and the ball landing on red. He enjoyed watching hotel security escort enraged gamblers out of the casino as they screamed idle threats at him.

It didn't take long for the gaming authorities to sniff out the scam at the Golden Horseshoe, which made Bernrd Red an offer he couldn't refuse. They gave him his degree in Hotel Management, they set him up as a concierge in a bed-and-breakfast on a road called Bath in a seaside village out West, and they told him never to come back.

On Bernrd Red's last day in Las Vegas, the casino owner gave him a pinky ring with a giant ruby as an expression of his gratitude. He patted Bernrd Red on the back, winked an avuncular wink, and said, "Always bet on Red."

18. You, Your Best Friend, and Your Vilest Enemy

During his time in the asylum, Zachary R. was visited by Bernrd Red, which is to say that the grudge he held against Bernrd Red manifested itself in the form of imaginary visits. The first such visit went like this:

Zachary R. sat up in bed in the asylum listening to the Electric Light Dirge for Cello and Organ, when Bernrd Red entered the room.

Bernrd Red despised music. Zachary R. hit pause and asked, "Would you like to sit with me and listen to this lovely dirge?"

Bernrd Red replied, "If you don't turn off the music, I am going to betray you, your best friend, and your vilest enemy."

"Looks like you get to fuck yourself three times, then," said Zachary R.

The two men fought feebly. Asylum staff separated them. Zachary R. was placed in isolation. His mowing privileges were suspended.

19. Bigger Moths Need Bigger Flames

When their first son, Bernrd Red, was sent west to become a self-styled cooler at the Golden Horseshoe in Las Vegas (and later a malevolent concierge at a bed-and-breakfast on a road called Bath in a seaside village), his parents, the well-to-do and good-for-nothing banker, H. Charles Branhoover, and the roughhouse prostitute, Chloe Red, decided it was okay at last, that it wouldn't ruin Branhoover's reputation in the banking industry, for them to formally announce their mutual admiration by getting married.

Of course, as is often the case, the only two people in all of Pittsburgh who believed their version of the story of their relationship were H. Charles and Chloe Red themselves.

And so they got married and Pittsburgh went along with the whole apparatus of their farce. And then Mrs. Chloe Branhoover announced she was pregnant with the couple's "first" child, who, if a girl, would be called Hilda Janice Branhoover and, if a boy, Haley James Branhoover.

H. James Branhoover, the Branhoover's second son, was born on a thin autumn Sunday. He was raised like a prince and he behaved like one, too. He ran away to Hollywood because bigger moths need bigger flames, and he leapt to his death from the roof of a youth hostel.

PART III

20. The Wrinkles Around Your Eyes

One night, during the days and nights leading up to his committal, Zachary R. dreamt about a Red Cross nurse in a nun's habit. In the dream, she motioned for him to follow. Fog passed above and diagonally. He looked at her and asked, "What do you want me to do?" Because she also wore a veil, he could not interpret her reply. He awoke thinking about the Cold Angel.

He arrived at work that morning lit by the black sun of empathy, thinking "Service to mankind, Service to mankind." He took the elevator to the top floor, to his station in the file room, where he clocked in and settled down. Then he took the elevator down one floor to the litigation department, where he made a photocopy. The lines of his hands appeared along the blackened edges, reminding him of the wrinkles around the nurse's eyes. He looked at the floor and tightened his lips in sad reflection.

But the sound of others working their machines scintillated his brain:

Keyboards clicking. Phones ringing. The mechanics of a bustling office. Graves being dug in the continents of the world.

So the nurse asked, "Is that a map of the New Hampshire mountains you're copying?"

And he replied, "How did you access my brain?"

"It was you who accessed my brain," she said. "So, when did you decide to quit your job and save the world?"

And he said, "I decided here at this copier, while thinking about the wrinkles around your eyes."

21. The Cold Angel

When the Cold Angel was alive on Earth, she was a Red Cross nurse who traveled widely in service to mankind.

She cried a lot and suffered from insomnia, which deepened the wrinkles around her eyes and lowered her core temperature a full degree below normal, to 97.6 degrees Fahrenheit.

She died of malaria in the jungle of Southeast Asia, the parasitic protozoa of the disease occupying and destroying her red blood corpuscles. The bitter irony of such a fate for a Red Cross nurse did not escape her, nor did her hatred of mosquitoes, which she took with her into the afterlife and which gave her the power to summon and control the movement of fog, which reminded her of smoke, which repelled the disease-carrying insects.

The Cold Angel's feelings toward Zachary R. were ambivalent. On the one hand, she felt motherly pity for him on account of his naïve and compassionate nature, which she displayed herself and which was a prerequisite for a life in service to mankind. On the other hand, these were the same qualities about him that she despised. There is a certain ignorant arrogance, a narcissism in those who believe they have the power to change things for the better. The Cold Angel was convinced that it was these qualities which made her cry, lowered her temperature, and caused her to suffer a horrific death in the jungle.

She could see that Zachary R. was likely to suffer her fate, so she came to comfort him and to send him on his mission, which she hoped would show him his folly and reform him before it was too late.

22. Red Cross Nurse in a Nun's Habit

When the Cold Angel was alive on Earth, her first mission to Southeast Asia in service to mankind was to a primitive village in the Philippines. The inhabitants there were suspicious of Western medicine but not of Western religion, so in order to gain their trust, the Red Cross nurses wore nuns' habits with crucifixes rather than the all-white uniforms with bright red Red Cross crosses.

The Cold Angel met with such tremendous success in the village, inoculating the children and teaching good hygiene, that she took to wearing the nun's habit on all of her missions, including Thailand, Vietnam, Cambodia, and Laos, even gaining recognition for her tireless service from the Vatican and Mother Teresa.

It was not long before the Cold Angel converted to Catholicism, took her vows, and became a bona fide nun.

When asked—after her death—to describe the Cold Angel, the sisters in her convent firmly and unanimously asserted their belief that she was headed for sainthood. They considered the drop of her core temperature to be a sign, perhaps even a precursor to the miracle of the stigmata, which they all hoped for dearly, checking her hands and feet each morning for wounds, which they never found, except for the mosquito bites that she suffered frequently and which eventually led to her death by malaria.

As the Red Cross nurse in a nun's habit lay dying, she prayed to God for one more mission in service to mankind. Her prayer was not answered, but it wasn't ignored altogether. God, that bald family man, rewarded her in the afterlife by making her a shivering angel, called the Cold Angel, complete with veil, hands like winter, and the power to summon and control the movement of fog, all in service to mankind, which meant in service to Zachary R.

23. The Goth Girls

The Goth Girls gathered once a century in the cathedrals, prisons, and streets of the world to select a troubled man to torment and to protect.

Having wearied of tormenting and protecting a well-known German composer in the eighteenth century, in the nineteenth century they opted for John Brown of Harpers Ferry. Not only did they admire his violent piety, which is five-fourths of pity, but also they were attracted to his paranoid hair and to how he complemented the pillory.

In the twentieth century, they selected Harry Houdini, for not only did they admire his malevolence toward the claustrophobic, but also they swooned to the song of his name.

In the twenty-first century, they wanted a joker, a man who ate numbers off apartment doors, a man who spoke to a cracked snail in the searing mental sun, a man who refused sex because he thought it would diminish his chances of becoming a Messiah or Rock Star. But mainly they wanted a man who made them giggle.

That man was Zachary R.

Their selection was made on a thin autumn Friday, the day before his committal, the day when Zachary R. coughed blood into the toilet and it formed the shape of a rose.

PART IV

24. Like Negligent Acupuncture

On the corner of the street of the twilit bungalow was a pole dedicated to a button dedicated to the regulation of traffic.

A seven-year-old Zachary R. pressed that button and pressed it again just to be sure. The woman in front of him, his mother, turned in her tissue-fiber nightgown and said, "I already pressed the button and you knew that, but you pressed it again anyway."

She reached for a knitting needle, which protruded from a rip in her bag.

"You looked like you were waiting for a train," he said, "to hop on a boxcar. That's why you forgot to press the button."

She clinched the needle and winced like negligent acupuncture when it punctured a bag of birdseed, spilling the contents onto the sidewalk to the delight of pigeons and Goth Girls, who were searching for a joker to torment and to protect.

"Just kidding," he said. "Sometimes I have to press the button no matter what. I apologize."

Her chin dropped and her eyes widened with approval. An entry was made in the Book of Do's and Don'ts.

25. The Book of Do's and Don'ts

Zachary R.'s mother's frayed nerves were caused by her encounters with the Book of Do's and Don'ts, to which she was made privy in her dreams.

The book was three-by-five feet and was kept in Argos, Greece, in the exact center of an all-marble edifice with an opening in the roof that allowed a pillar of light to shine down upon the open pages.

Each night when Zachary R.'s mother went to bed, she did so fearfully yet unaware that she would face a full accounting of the day's do's and don'ts.

The Book of Do's and Don'ts was not a book of rules. Rather, it was a running commentary on the main events with moral implications which occurred on that day. For example, the entry made on the day when her son pressed the button and she winced like negligent acupuncture, was as follows:

Do's	Don'ts
1. Wearing your tissue-fiber nightgown in public. Who cares what the neighbors think?	1. Getting irritated with your son when he pressed the button, even though he knew you had already pressed it. He's just a mischievous boy, after all.
2. Explaining to your son why you were irritated with him. You	2. Wearing your tissue-fiber nightgown in public. You should

should always have a reason for being upset with him. You should never be upset with him "just because." Well done.	care about the negative consequences this could have on your son.
3. Clinching the knitting needle and wincing like negligent acupuncture when it punctured your bag of birdseed, spilling the contents onto the sidewalk. Not only did this feed hungry pigeons, but also it made your son laugh at you and then feel bad about it, which made him apologize for pressing the button.	3. Clinching the knitting needle. Don't threaten to stab your son over such a minor offense. Actually, don't ever threaten to stab him.

4. Accepting your son's apology, showing him your approval with your widened eyes. You really can be a good mother sometimes.	

When Zachary R.'s mother awoke in the morning, her nerves were shot, but she couldn't determine why.

26. The Twilit Bungalow

In the days and nights leading up to his committal, Zachary R. spent the hours in reverie at work and then, after he quit, along the rivers and tributaries and seashore of Massachusetts, and finally in the mountains of New Hampshire.

He wore a heavy coat and bit into a bad burger in a shed along the riverbank.

He made photocopies in a skyscraper. He crouched under a table that pine cones bounced off of. He walked the aisle of a hardware store and reached into a barrel of nails that rattled and brushed his spine like silk, urging him to nap.

Job was lost. Wife was cremated. Pram did not squeak.

He believed in the morning. He believed in Messiahs and Rock Stars. He believed he could still be one or the other, or both at the same time. He believed he was on a mission to save the world.

But there was also the childhood memory of the twilit bungalow with sunflowers painted thick on the mailbox and grease stains on the driveway and tires propped against a chain-link fence and a parrot out of its cage that shit on the kitchen stove and his chess-obsessed father and his mother and her frayed nerves and tissue-fiber nightgown lying in bed for three years straight

and her young son who gazed out the living room
window fogged in breath that said, "I want to
take some kind of endless train."

27. The Book of Do's and Don'ts

An entry was made in the Book of Do's and
Don'ts concerning the twilit bungalow, to wit:

Do's	Don'ts
1. Providing a twilit bungalow with sunflowers painted thick on the mailbox. The home that you and your chess-obsessed husband have provided for your son has created a sense of security for him, albeit tenuous. He	1. Providing a twilit bungalow with sunflowers painted thick on the mailbox. Why do you and your chess-obsessed husband insist on keeping your home in a state of perpetual dimness? This quirk of yours is

also secretly loves the sunflowers on the mailbox, because they remind him of a van Gogh painting he saw in a book.	liable to drive your son nuts. Also, the sunflowers on the mailbox are poorly rendered in comparison to the van Gogh painting your son saw in a book.
2. Having grease stains on the driveway and tires propped against a chain-link fence. It is essential for a family to have a car in this day and age. Good job.	2. Having grease stains on the driveway and tires propped against a chain-link fence. You neglect your car like you neglect your son. You are an awful mother.
	3. Allowing the parrot to be out of its cage to shit on the kitchen stove. No explanation should be necessary for

	this one.
	4. Lying in bed for three years straight. If you got out of bed, you would see your son gazing out the living room window, sick with worry that he is the cause of your condition. It will be a miracle if he doesn't wind up in a mental asylum someday.

When Zachary R.'s mother awoke in the morning, her head hurt and her mouth was dry, but she couldn't determine why.

28. Mother with Child in Subway

An eight-year-old Zachary R. stood on the shoulder of a foggy road waving his arms. A traveler saw him and pulled over. He grabbed the traveler's arm and led her to the place where his mother lay motionless. He reached for his mother's body and said, "I am afraid to die." The traveler felt for a pulse and found one. She told him not to worry, that his mother was alive. She considered asking him why he said, "I am afraid to die" rather than, "Please don't die," but she decided it would be better to remain silent. When he stopped shaking, she asked him what had happened. Zachary R. told the traveler that his mother was showing him how to climb a pine tree when a pine cone came loose and fell, bouncing loudly off a picnic table, startling her, and causing her to fall. The traveler believed this explanation, but it was a lie. The truth was that he had been linking together boxcar after boxcar on an imaginary train that he said went forever through tunnels in hills with shacks and cigarettes. He said it was an endless train that never stopped. This made so little sense to his mother that she suffered a nervous breakdown and collapsed unconscious on the hard dirt.

Either way, the only truth that mattered was the truth of his injured mother, who had taken the boy to the New Hampshire mountains to get him away from chess, from his father. The traveler realized that she wouldn't be able to lift the boy's mother, so she retrieved a sleeping bag from the trunk of her car, lay it next to the woman, rolled her onto it, and then dragged her to the car, where the two of them managed to slide her onto the backseat. The traveler instructed Zachary R. to sit in the back with his mother, who was now conscious. Zachary R. said he was sorry about the endless train, but his mother just moaned and glared. The traveler, sensing the tension, rummaged through the suitcase on the passenger seat and pulled out her family album. She handed the album to

Zachary R. He looked intently at each photo, but the one he liked best was a photo of a boy and his mother alone in a subway train. He pulled the photo out of its pocket and looked at the back. The inscription read, "Mother with Child in Subway."

29. The Book of Do's and Don'ts

An entry was made in the Book of Do's and Don'ts concerning the incident in the New Hampshire mountains, to wit:

Do's	Don'ts
1. Taking your son to the New Hampshire mountains to get him away from chess, from his father. It was decent of you to notice	1. Suffering a nervous breakdown and collapsing on the hard dirt when your boy described the endless train. This just in:

the stress that chess and your husband were causing your boy, but perhaps you took him to the mountains because of the stress that chess and your husband were causing you. In any event, there should be at least one entry in the Do's column, so here it is.	Young boys have wild imaginations, which should be encouraged, not discouraged. A nervous breakdown? You cannot be serious.
	2. Moaning and glaring when your son said sorry about the endless train. Your son's apology was sincere, and you knew this. Why didn't you accept his apology? And really, did he need to apologize for

	having an imagination?
	3. Forcing your son to find a surrogate mother in the photograph in the traveler's family album. This is the equivalent of telling him his only viable option for survival in this world is to be saved by zero.
	4. Have you noticed that, once again, there are more don'ts than do's? This by itself qualifies as a don't.

When Zachary R.'s mother awoke in the morning, her chest was tight and she could barely breathe, but she couldn't determine why.

30. You Can Be Married and Still Die of Loneliness

Compassion is the method, convergence is the goal.

This was Zachary R.'s unspoken mantra during his childhood. Unspoken because he was a quiet boy who acted on principle, even if he couldn't articulate what the principle was.

His parents could see that he wanted them to be together and happy. And they were together, if together meant living in the same house.

The rumor was that Mr. and Mrs. R. had come together three times. Once on their first date—there was no Internet back then and neither of them was given to writing letters. Twice on their wedding day—Mr. R. looked at the imminent Mrs. R. and recited the words. Mrs. R. did the same. Mr. R. kissed Mrs. R.'s wincing face, though his mind was on knights, rooks, and bishops. Thrice when Mr. and Mrs. R. converged to create Zachary R. When Zachary R. was released from his mother's womb, he was placed in the maternity ward and then driven home by his parents, who, though they lived in the same house, went their separate ways.

The three of them lived in the twilit bungalow, but Mr. R. spent all of his time in the game room, which was dedicated to one game, chess. Mrs. R. dedicated her time to receding into the neurosis of her recurring nightmare—the Book of Do's and Don'ts—of which she was entirely unaware.

Zachary R. would come between them, sweetly, delicately, and say things like, "What time is dinner tonight?"

Or, "Mom and Dad, come look at the endless train I am building myself."

Mr. R.'s exclusive response was to grunt and shut the game room door, which was painted in sixty-four black and white squares, like minor concussions.

Mrs. R.'s customary response was to poke her head out her bedroom door and say, "It is so obvious what you are up to" and then vanish into bed in her tissue-fiber nightgown.

Zachary R.'s only company in the twilit bungalow was the parrot out of its cage that shit on the kitchen stove and his own imagination, which conjured up boxcars and the endless train that went through tunnels in hills with shacks and cigarettes.

Sometimes his mother would come out of her room to check on the boy, but mainly she wanted to see him to test out her pitiful cries for attention, such as, "You can be married and still die of loneliness."

Zachary R.'s response to such things was to knock on his father's door and ask if he wanted to play chess, which he always did.

31. The Book of Don'ts

An entry was made in the Book of Do's and Don'ts concerning Mrs. R.'s remarks to her son, to wit:

Don'ts
1. Notice anything different about this entry? No doubt, you can see that there is only one column this time. Awful. Just awful.
2. Saying, "It is so obvious what you are up to" in response to your son's compassionate attempt to unite the family. Indeed, it *is* obvious what he is up to, which should make it all the more easy for you to find a way to come together. But instead, you would rather shut the door on him and go lie on your pressure sores.
3. Saying, "You can be married and still die of loneliness" in a pathetic plea for

sympathy. I've got news for you. You're not the one in need of sympathy. Your son is, and you know it. Maybe he would be better off without you.

When morning arrived, Zachary R.'s mother did not awake. Her body wasn't discovered until three days later, when Zachary R. knocked on his father's door and the two of them went into her bedroom in silence, sensing that something was wrong. When Mr. R. explained to Zachary R. that his mother was gone, the boy began to sob at the foot of the bed, saying over and over, "It's my fault. It's all my fault."

Mr. R. took the young Zachary R. in his arms and stroked his hair, assuring him that it wasn't his fault at all. Then he carried Zachary R. into the game room, where the two of them fell asleep seated on fold-out chairs on opposite ends of a chessboard.

The next morning Mr. R. made funeral arrangements for his wife.

32. My Job Is to Father You

At the funeral of Mrs. R., Mr. R. searched his mind for a way to comfort his son, who was still convinced that he caused her death. Zachary R. sobbed on and on about the boxcars and the endless train being why his mother was dead. Finally, Mr. R. said, "Listen, son. I've been thinking about why your mother died. She died because she loved you so much that it paralyzed her, made it impossible for her to do anything. So it's nobody's fault. Do you see? And I know if she could be here now, she would say she loved you and that it wasn't your fault."

Zachary R. looked directly at his father and said, "You won't be paralyzed, right, Dad? Because of chess. Right?"

"That's right, Zachary. Chess makes me strong. But I love you too, just like your mother did."

"But if you love me as much as she did, then why aren't you paralyzed?"

"I do love you as much as your mother did, Zachary, but my job isn't to mother you, my job is to father you."

"And fathers don't get paralyzed because they know how to play chess?" asked Zachary.

"You're damn right," said Zachary R.'s father.

PART V

33. Mustard All Over Your Face

Pawn takes pawn. Bishop takes pawn. Knight takes bishop.

A fourteen-year-old Zachary R. surveyed the midgame chessboard. His mind was supposed to be on his first junior chess tournament, which was forthcoming, but he was thinking about prisons and cathedrals instead.

His father had just made his move and was now in the kitchen frying hamburgers while keeping an eye on his son's hand as it jerked over the pieces. His father went from stove to fridge to cutting board, creeping like a critic hoping to be offended.

Zachary R. made his move. Knight takes bishop.

His father's eyes widened with approval. He placed the burgers on the buns, making small circles of mustard in the exact center of each.

"Excellent move, Zachary," he said. "I believe you'll have checkmate in less than ten moves. Have a burger."

Zachary R. leaned back in his chair and took a medium bite. A dab of mustard squirted out the corner of his mouth, leaving a small yellow stain on his pubescent face, his right-angle chin at sixty degrees and growing.

His father's expression changed from approval to disgust. "You've got mustard all over your face," he said.

Zachary R. knocked the burgers and the chess pieces off the table and ran down the street toward the hill of shacks and cigarettes, where he waited impossibly for an endless train.

34. Hit in the Head by a Pebble

Zachary R. lay in bed in the asylum thinking about how he threw away certain victory because of his fault-finding, embellishing father.

Bernrd Red shined a flashlight into the room and said, "Don't embellish on his embellishments. At least this isn't a story about a boy and his dog."

Zachary R. couldn't disagree with this statement. For once, Bernrd Red was promoting the sensation of being hit in the head by a pebble, rather than a rock.

The two men talked almost cordially for several minutes, and even though Zachary R. still was unable to convince Bernrd Red of the merits of music, he did get him to remove the ring from his pinky.

And then something very uncharacteristic, even inspiring, happened. Bernrd Red gave Zachary R. a bear hug. But it wasn't clear to Zachary R. whether the hug was malevolent or affectionate. The hug was malevolent, as Bernrd Red slipped the ring back on his pinky behind Zachary R.'s back.

Zachary R. wheezed to regain depleted oxygen.

He rolled his neck.

The bees and bones inside him buzzed and popped with such force that he fell asleep drooling.

35. Scholar's Mate

White's opening moves: king's pawn to e4, queen to h5, king's bishop to c4, queen to f7.

Checkmate in four moves, a scholar's mate, for Zachary R. in the opening match of his first junior chess tournament.

His father grunted and shook his fist in the air.

Zachary R.'s opponent, a meek child, began to cry.

Zachary R. quickly moved his chair aside, walked around the table, and put his hand on the child's shoulder.

"Don't worry," said Zachary R. "My dad checkmated me like that the first time I played him. I promise, after if happens to you the first time, it will never happen again. You'll see it coming a mile away."

Zachary R. smiled. The meek child smiled back.

This was Zachary R.'s first experience lit by the black sun of empathy.

Suddenly Zachary R. felt the jarring thud of his father's hand as it wrapped around his small bicep and pulled him out of the tournament room.

"Well done, son," said Zachary R.'s father. "Don't let it go to your head. And don't talk to your opponent after the match. It's poor form."

"Yes, sir," said Zachary R.

"Don't call me sir, Zachary. This isn't the army."

"Okay, Dad."

So much information. Too much of it confusing. The messages: You played well, but don't feel too good about it; it's poor form to talk to your opponent after the match even if it obviously made him feel better; this isn't the army, I'm ordering you not to behave as if it were.

36. The Black Sun of Empathy

The black sun of empathy is black because it operates on the inside. It is sun because it produces light and heat.

The black sun of empathy operates on the principles of "do unto others as you would have others do unto you"; "the needs of the many outweigh the needs of the few"; "from each according to his ability, to each according to his need"; "boy, you're gonna carry that weight a long time"; and, "the purpose of life is to die saving someone else's life."

Many famous and heroic men and women followed the principles of the black sun of empathy. None of them lived long, to wit: Gandhi, Martin Luther King, Jr., Joan of Arc, Jack and Bobby Kennedy, Benazir Bhutto, John Lennon, Jesus.

Zachary R. experienced the black sun of empathy and, like Joan of Arc, he also spent time under the searing mental sun.

37. Fool's Mate

The opening moves: White f3, black e5. White g4, black Qh4.

Checkmate in two moves, a fool's mate, for Zachary R.'s opponent in the semifinals of Zachary R.'s first junior chess tournament.

Zachary R.'s father grunted, shook his fist at his son and walked out of the room. Zachary R.'s opponent, an arrogant child, tormented Zachary R. as Zachary stood up to reach across the table to shake the child's hand.

"How did you manage to make it all the way to the semifinals?" asked the child. "Guess your side of the draw was for retards."

"Can't you see that I let you win?" replied Zachary R.

"Yeah right, fool's mate," said the child.

Zachary R. yanked the arrogant child across the table by his handshaking hand, scattering the pieces and dragging him to the tournament floor, frantically punching his ears and forehead.

Tournament officials quickly descended on Zachary R. and pulled him off of the arrogant child, who had pissed his trousers because of the shocking ferocity of Zachary R.'s attack.

This was Zachary R.'s first experience under the searing mental sun.

38. The Searing Mental Sun

The searing mental sun was painted thick and blinding on the inside of Zachary R.'s skull, like the sunflowers on the mailbox of the twilit bungalow, like the van Gogh painting he saw in a book. And the thick and blinding paint dripped from inside his skull and colored his mind searing yellow, the intensity of which made it impossible for him to keep his balance, caused him to tilt and moan and draw spirals that became portraits of the Cracked Snail.

The searing mental sun and the black sun of empathy mixed together to misguide Zachary R., who did both good and bad like everyone else.

39. No Pontius Pilate

Zachary R. was so naïve and disconnected, so cut off from himself and others, so compassionate, so self-obsessed and sexy with his right-angle chin, that even when he had ulterior motives, he was the last to know.

This meant he could genuinely believe he was acting calm and kind, but friends, family, and bystanders could plainly see he was calmly and kindly sharpening an axe with a tilted stare.

In other words, Zachary R. was no Pontius Pilate.

There was no Roman rationalization in his eyes.

No imperial impropriety in his heart.

No washbasin for his bloody hands.

In other words, Zachary R. was bad at politics.

Indeed, there was an infuriating innocence to him that friends, family, and bystanders found more offensive than an axe to the head. "It is so obvious what you are up to," they would say.

It was as if they had been banished to his Bethlehem in their Las Vegas state of mind.

40. Messiah or Rock Star

Zachary R.'s childhood ended with the death of his mother. He forced himself to forget about the boxcars and the endless train that went through tunnels in hills with shacks and cigarettes. He lied to his father and agreed that his mother's death wasn't his fault, even though he still believed it was. He dutifully continued to play in all the chess tournaments his dad signed him up for, doing well enough to get noticed by his middle school and then his high school.

Zachary R. was one of the region's best junior chess players, but chess wasn't the only reason Zachary R. got noticed in middle school and in high school. Another reason Zachary R. got noticed was that his confidence grew, which caused the girls to giggle, which motivated him to buy a guitar with the money he earned helping at his mother's church, where the pastor had instilled in Zachary R.'s mother an acute sense of right and wrong, of the do's and don'ts of life, as he liked to call them.

Zachary R. never told the pastor about the boxcars and the endless train and the incident in the forest in the New Hampshire mountains that drove his mother into her tissue-fiber nightgown and into bed forever. He never explained that he went to church in search of forgiveness for that incident, which in his mind led to her demise. And so the pastor mistakenly believed that Zachary R. was just an uncommonly devout young man, like Jesus himself. And the pastor became like Paul to Zachary and mentored the boy on the do's and don'ts of life, as he liked to call them.

The pastor told Zachary R. that he had what it took to be like Jesus, his devotion to service and his highly developed sense of empathy toward his chess opponents being two of his finest qualities. But along with the do's came the don'ts. The pastor explained to Zachary R. that if he continued in his service to the church that he could change the world, but if he wanted to change the world, he would have to avoid the temptations of the world, and by temptations, the pastor meant sexual relations with the ever-growing number of young women who, the pastor noticed, were paying attention to his young disciple.

The pastor called Zachary R. to his office and said, "You're not interested in all that, are you?"

"I'm sorry," said Zachary R. "I'm afraid I don't understand what you mean."

"I mean those girls you're talking to," said the pastor. "There must be at least seven of them."

"I'm not doing anything wrong," said Zachary R.

The pastor stretched out both of his arms and put both of his hands on Zachary R.'s shoulders. "Not yet, Zachary," he said. "But if you want to be like Jesus, you have to refuse to have sex with those girls. Having sex outside of marriage is a don't, Zachary."

Zachary R. lay in bed that night, tense as a gargoyle and unbearably awake because of what the pastor had told him. But after hours of deliberation, he decided he would stop flirting with the girls in order to increase his chances of becoming a Messiah or Rock Star, which, if he succeeded, would absolve him of the sin of his mother's death.

Insomnia troubled Zachary R. until dawn, when at last he slept for an hour, then awoke erect as a saint with no one to touch.

41. Rock 'n' Roll High School

Under the tutelage of his father and the pastor, Zachary R. became one of the most disciplined and successful kids at his high school, becoming a confident student and chess player, and refusing sex with the seven or so young women who would have been willing or even agreeable to having sex with him.

One girl in particular, a kind and unassuming redhead with typical redhead features—fair skin, pale blue eyes, and a sensitive, colorful, energetic personality—took a keen interest in Zachary R. and had her girlfriend show him a family photo in which she thought she looked pretty. The girlfriend showed Zachary R. the photo in math class and innocently asked him what he thought about the girl on the end in the green dress.

Zachary R. said, "I recognize her. She's in my English class. I think she's gorge—I mean, I think she's somewhat gorgeous, that chess is nearly impossible." Zachary R. felt the twofold pain of lying and denying his true feelings. He felt sharp melancholic daggers in his stomach and heart.

The girlfriend frowned and put the photo back into her backpack. Her opinion of Zachary R. diminished significantly with that remark, which was unlucky for him, since she was popular and a gossip.

News got around that Zachary R. was stuck up and a chicken, yet many students still admired him from a distance due to his imperviousness to their overt antipathy toward him, his clean lifestyle, his unswerving faith, his good grades, his success at chess, and his guitar prowess. They saw him as aloof and above their petty criticisms, which only increased their pettiness and his aloofness.

The pastor, on the other hand, was pleased with Zachary R. and explained to him that Jesus, too, was misunderstood and even hated in his time. Zachary R. was glad to know his chances for Messiah or Rock Star, for his mother's forgiveness, were intact.

The girls who once liked him, and especially the redhead, who was heartbroken but still had a high opinion of him, were baffled as Zachary R. withdrew and his appearance and personality became less and less attractive. These same girls, and even the redhead, began to pay attention to the other boys, which frustrated Zachary R. and made him suffer under the searing mental sun.

Despite his talent at guitar, he lost any desire to start a band. He began to talk to himself in class, which got him sent to the school psychiatrist. He lost all patience for chess and started to lose, which irritated his father, who stopped speaking to him entirely.

His grades suffered, but not enough to prevent him from graduating. And graduate he did, but he refused to attend the graduation ceremony. Instead, he informed the school psychiatrist that he wanted his diploma mailed.

He thought about running away to Hollywood to start a band out there, but this was just a thought.

The summer after high school, Zachary R.'s father gave him three months to find a job, saying that come September, job or no job, he was kicking him out of the house.

Zachary R. moved out in July when he landed a file clerk position at the Law Offices of Miller & Associates, where they happily employed the organizational skills he had gleaned from chess and the discipline he had learned from the pastor of his mother's church.

Zachary R. lived the first years of his twenties like a monk, until he saw his future wife asleep in the hall with the blue carpet.

42. Stuffed and Perched in a Cage

While it is not exactly clear what happened to Zachary R.'s father, it is widely believed that he happily lived out the rest of his days at his local chess club and in the game room of the twilit bungalow, where he had his wife's parrot stuffed and, at last, perched in a cage.

43. The Book of Do's

Soon after Zachary R. found a job and took an apartment, he quit chess, guitar, and church. But, the three did not quit him. And he spent his days in three places, too—at home, going to and from work, and at work itself. As far as going to and from work was concerned, Zachary R. rode the bus, and later, after he had saved enough money, he purchased and drove the Nova.

And in all three places he spent more and more time in the searing mental sun. He no longer played chess, but he saw chess pieces in everything. He no longer played guitar, but his love of music grew. He especially liked the requiems of Mozart, Fauré, and Richafort, and the Electric Light Dirge for Cello and Organ by an obscure American composer.

He no longer attended church, but he did not give up on the dream of becoming a Messiah or Rock Star. On one night in particular, he dreamt of a cathedral in Bethlehem that had a telescope where the rose window should have been and he climbed a ladder and looked through the telescope, which saw all the way to a marble edifice in Argos, Greece, and he looked down an opening in the roof that allowed in a pillar of light that illuminated the open pages of a three-by-five-foot book called the Book of Do's and Don'ts. Though he could not see her, he could hear his dead mother begging the Book to leave her alone, and he saw the one entry in the Book that was intended for him, to wit:

Do's
1. Go in search of rivers and women. The rest is meaningless.

Zachary R. awoke in the morning feeling good for the first time in his life, but he couldn't determine why.

PART VI

44. You Smell Like Rain

Zachary R. first noticed Annabel R. asleep on the blue carpet in the common hall of his first apartment. He stared at her for a long time and the longer he stared, the more his mind emptied.

His troubles floated in the vacuum of her dormant image. He nudged her awake and said, "You smell like rain."

Her eyes twitched, opened a little, then closed again.

Zachary R. went back to his room and forgot what she looked like, but he wondered about the inside of her apartment and what might happen if he spent time with her there.

45. The Blue Carpet in the Hall

The first time Zachary R. saw Annabel R. asleep on the blue carpet in the hall was not the first time she had slept there. Annabel R. had just been kicked out of her father's house, and moved into her own apartment, where she acted out the story of "The Little Match Girl." The blue carpet in the hall reminded her of the cold Danish alleyway where the little girl struck the matches and saw visions before she died.

Now Annabel R. lay on the blue carpet and pretended to freeze to death, pretended to see visions, pretended that if she came home without money, her father would beat her, which essentially wasn't pretend, except for the fact that money had nothing to do with it.

The first time Annabel R. had a real vision on the blue carpet was the first time Zachary R. noticed her there, his mind emptying, his troubles floating in the vacuum of her dormant image.

She dreamt that it was the vernal equinox and a young man with eyes that blossomed like sunflowers invited her to the carnival.

When she awoke, there he was just staring at her until finally he said, "You smell like rain."

Annabel R. thought, "I am going to know this man and it is going to be important."

She thought about what she liked about him that wasn't sentimental . . . That she dreamt him before she met him. No. Sentimental. That his eyes blossomed like sunflowers. Better, but still sentimental. That he noticed she smelled like rain. Made her heart leap, but still sentimental. That when she woke and saw him staring at her, he didn't speak for an uncomfortable length of time. That was it. Zachary R. was mostly silent. That was what she liked most about him.

Annabel R. wrote "Mostly Silent" on a matchbook and slipped it under his door.

46. Mostly Silent

Annabel R. knew she was going to know Zachary R. and it was going to be important. She slid a matchbook under his door with the words "Mostly Silent" written on it, which was, by Zachary R.'s underdeveloped sense of romance, the most bewitching of surprises.

But the vernal equinox was fast approaching and Zachary R. hadn't so much as uttered a hello, let alone knocked on her door and formally introduced himself.

But this didn't mean Zachary R. wasn't interested. On the contrary, he was so smitten with the mysterious sleeping match girl in the hall with the blue carpet that he was devising a strategy not just for a first date, but also for a way to get her into his life for the long term.

On March 18, he thought, "Should I bring her flowers? No. Too common." On March 19, "Dinner and a movie? No. She is too original to be impressed by such gestures."

And then, on March 20, the day before the vernal equinox, Zachary R. saw a band of gypsy kids posting small poster ads for the carnival, which was to stake a patch of earth at the foot of the hill of shacks and cigarettes and open on March 21.

Zachary R. liked the carnival. He lay awake all night hoping that when morning came, he would see Annabel R. in the hall with the blue carpet.

47. The Carnival

Wheels and ropes. Beetles and straw. Logs and parachutes. Sage and thaw.

The next morning Zachary R. saw Annabel R. in the hallway with the blue carpet, but this time she was awake, leaning against the wall, following the path of the sunlight as it moved along the opposite wall.

He stared at her until she said, "Today is the vernal equinox. What are you doing?" He opened his backpack and showed her a small poster ad for the carnival, which had staked a patch of earth at the foot of the hill of shacks and cigarettes.

She went back inside her apartment for a moment and reappeared in a burgundy dress. Her hair was parted down the middle.

Zachary R. wore an indigo T-shirt and sideburns, which complemented his right-angle chin. His eyes blossomed like sunflowers.

They set off on foot toward the patch of earth that the carnival had roped and logged, beetled and strawed. They joined a procession of coolers, crows, and firecrackers, and in less than an hour they arrived.

Colors flashed. The grand wheel spun. Hot dogs rolled on metal rods. Paper cups and wrappers blew over shoes and ants.

At the carnival Zachary R. felt vital to the mechanics of the world. He looked deeply into Annabel's eyes, but she did not kiss him.

Instead, she led him to the photo booth by the fortune teller. She sat him down and drew the curtain. No photos were taken.

They rode the parachutes. They fired guns. They burned sage in the name of loneliness, but it was so warm that the sky seemed to descend and nothing was distant.

Zachary and Annabel moved through the carnival in such gentle oblivion that gypsy kids had no trouble stealing rolls of tickets from their pockets.

48. The Photo Booth and the Brass Knuckles of Sex

Zachary R. did not object to sex in the photo booth, especially since Annabel's dress concealed the mechanics of the act. What was surprising was that they occupied the booth for twenty minutes and no one drew back the curtain, not even the gypsy kids. Most likely all of the carnival patrons were conditioned to recognize the piston-like sound of the working parts and elected out of empathy to direct their attention toward the fortune teller.

Either way, Annabel became pregnant with Sarah R. And, of almost equal importance, conception occurred in the photo booth rather than later that night in Annabel's apartment, because the sex that occurred in Annabel's apartment was hell compared to the sex at the carnival, which wasn't quite heaven, but was close.

Back in Annabel's apartment, Annabel ordered Zachary R. to sit on her bed while she retrieved a cigar box from the floor of the closet. She sat down beside him and opened the box, which contained brass knuckles and a romance novel called *Savage Splendor*. She ordered him to strike her with the brass knuckles while she read from the book. The sunflowers in his eyes wilted, but he obeyed. He struck her harder than she anticipated, which frenzied her and made her whirl and pop. Love came and went.

Zachary R. turned gray and began to weep. Annabel R. put her hand on his shoulder and fell asleep.

49. Solstices and Equinoxes

Morning sickness. Minor concussion. Birth of Sarah. Postpartum depression.

In the early days after the carnival, Annabel fell ill. At first, she thought it was the familiar aftereffects of the ritual beating she had received during sex: brass knuckles, *Savage Splendor*, and the ensuing concussion and nausea.

Then she remembered that her pregnancy test was positive and that the pregnancy was likely causing her morning sickness.

It was clear to both of them what needed to be done.

A wedding date was set for June 21, the summer solstice. This made sense from a romantic point of view (the carnival and the conception of Sarah R. occurred precisely on the vernal equinox) and a logical point of view (Annabel R. would not be showing at the end of the first trimester).

The honeymoon didn't immediately follow the wedding. Instead, because of the solstices and equinoxes, they decided to honeymoon the week of the autumnal equinox.

Sarah R. was born on December 21, the winter solstice, exactly nine months to the day after conception.

By now, the novelty of the solstices and equinoxes had worn thin. In fact, as Annabel R. held the newborn in her arms, she thought the baby was cursed. She fell into a deep postpartum depression for the rest of her days, which were numbered: seven hundred and thirty, to be exact.

50. Guests Dressed Up Like Dragons

Flash of bulb. Jet of plane. Swift of cloud. Drop of rain.

The wedding occurred on a wet summer Sunday of turbulent chairs and guests dressed up like dragons.

Zachary R. dressed up like a groom and made an appearance. Annabel R. was there too. He looked at her and recited the words. She did the same. He kissed her wincing face. Lights and noise were made when a jet flew over the ceremony. Zachary R. looked at the sky, his eyes blinking in the pinprick rain.

51. Frozen Little Girl

When she was little, Annabel liked to read, and she imagined herself downtrodden or orphaned, or both. She liked Hans Christian Andersen's "The Little Match Girl," especially the visions the little match girl had when she struck each match and also that the little match girl went to heaven to be with her grandmother and God when she died. On the other hand, Annabel had no tolerance for the sentimental and she held maudlin in contempt, so she made sure to keep the little match girl a secret by keeping a cigar box under the bed with a matchbook, a rag doll, and a locket with a photo of a pale boy called Damien, which she didn't care for, but she couldn't find a suitable photo of a frozen little girl.

Annabel R. guarded the cigar box and her sentimentality vigilantly.

Her father also kept a cigar box with secret contents. Photos of his wife, Annabel's mother, who had run away with a magician; photos of naked women and girls; and a pair of brass knuckles.

He demonstrated his love for his daughter using the contents of the cigar box. His daughter grew accustomed to her father's violent love, which fulfilled her downtrodden fantasy. She missed the ritual after high school ended and her father kicked her out.

In fact, on the day her father said goodbye, she pilfered the brass knuckles from his cigar box, placing them in her own cigar box along with a romance novel called *Savage Splendor*.

Annabel R. never set foot in her father's house again, but she continued her father's ritual with all of the boys and men in her life.

She went to the carnival with Zachary R. and conceived a child there. And back in her apartment that same night, she received her beating, which made her whirl and pop.

She cheated on Zachary R. with at least two men. And she received her beating from each of them.

PART VII

52. Lean Monday

Sarah R. spent all of Monday in her motel room in an apoplectic daze because she had scattered her mother's ashes across the lake. She sat on the floor at the foot of the bed, hugging the empty urn, trying to comprehend the finality of her actions.

She sobbed over the mother she never knew, who died when Sarah R. was two. She sobbed over her father, who was sick in a mental asylum and whom she had deceived.

She forgot to eat. She forgot to drink. She thought, "If tomorrow is Fat Tuesday, then today is Lean Monday."

Sarah R. fell asleep at dusk, still seated at the foot of the bed, still hugging the empty urn.

She woke at eleven thinking about the deadhead. She shaved her head, showered, threw on the Revolution Dress, and set off on foot to the Dungeon, where Mardi Gras began precisely at midnight.

53. Fat Tuesday; Ash Wednesday

Sarah R. spent the first six hours of Mardi Gras at the Dungeon, where the Dungeon Master poured her two-for-one drinks and listened attentively to her story about the deadhead from Kentucky.

The Dungeon Master, because he liked Sarah, didn't divulge the truth, which was that he knew the mysterious Kentuckian's identity. He was from out of town, it was true. But he was from just across the bridge in Mississippi and was a regular at the Dungeon until recently, because he was afraid of the possibility of running into a certain underage woman with a bald head who wore a burgundy dress that compelled him to utter words such as *adroit*, which he didn't know the meaning of but said anyway, as if the dress had coaxed the word out of him by some kind of voodoo.

Out of avuncular concern for Sarah, the Dungeon Master cut off her drinking privilege at six a.m. He kissed her on the cheek and sent her on her way toward Bourbon Street, which was already crowded with partiers who threw beads her way in recognition of her bald head and the Revolution Dress.

Suddenly, Sarah R. felt hungry. Because she didn't immediately see a hot dog cart, she opted for the nearest restaurant, a brightly lit twenty-four-hour diner.

The diner was so bright, in fact, that she had no trouble identifying the Kentuckian and his girlfriend sitting in one of the booths.

At that moment, the booze and the Revolution Dress took over.

"It's over, isn't it!?" she screamed at the deadhead.

The deadhead from Mississippi looked at his girlfriend with an expression that said, "I have no idea who this bald madgirl is."

What he did or didn't do was irrelevant to Sarah R. The crush was over.

She ran out of the diner and threw her beads into the street. The police on their horses paid no attention. She screamed obscenities at the languid trees. She cursed this city, this Necropolis, the Dungeon, the lake and its brackish voodoo, and the bright diner that had betrayed her.

She returned to her room, disrobed down to her bra and panties, and set fire to the Revolution Dress, which had also betrayed her.

When Sarah R. came to, it was to the face of a nurse with ash residue brushed across her forehead. The thought that she had died and gone to Hell for her bad deeds on Mardi Gras was quickly replaced by the thought that the day after Fat Tuesday is Ash Wednesday and that the nurse had just returned from church.

"Where am I?" asked Sarah R. cautiously.

The nurse didn't mince words. "You're in a hospital," she said. "You nearly burned down a motel last night."

Sarah R. winced. "What does the ash on your forehead mean?"

"Today is Ash Wednesday," said the nurse. "The first day of Lent. The ashes are an expression of sorrow for sins and a reminder that we are dust and will return to dust unless we repent and hear the good news."

"That's scary," said Sarah R. "I guess Fat Tuesday was my Ash Wednesday."

"Clever," said the nurse. "Not funny at all, but clever. You're lucky nobody got hurt in that motel you almost burned down."

But Sarah R. was no longer listening. She was thinking about all of the ashes in her young life. Her mother, the Revolution Dress, the motel, and even her father, who was returning to dust, slowly, with each passing day.

When the nurse left the room, the authorities entered and the interrogation began.

* * * * *

An entire week went by and Sarah R. was still in the hospital, but by now the authorities felt she had sufficiently regained her bearings and could return to society. She was reminded over and over that she had nearly burned down the bargain motel and that, luckily, nobody was seriously hurt.

During her stay in the hospital, Sarah R. told the authorities about her parents and where she lived, as the driver's license in her purse was a fake.

She told them about the descent of her father and the foreclosure on their house in New England.

She told them about the death of her mother and of scattering her mother's ashes across Lake Pontchartrain.

Because this was the state of Louisiana, and because there were many more Mardi Gras nutcases to be questioned, the only action the authorities took was to issue a citation for unauthorized disposal of human ashes into state waters. A hospital doctor prescribed a drug regimen of painkillers and antidepressants, and discharged her via wheelchair back onto the streets of New Orleans.

Sarah R. turned gray. She took her pills and staggered down the street to the nearest park, where she collapsed. The hot dog vendor knelt down beside her and emptied a bottled water from his cart onto her face to revive her.

She woke reluctantly, but the kind expression on the hot dog vendor's face made it easier for her to face consciousness and the truth about her predicament.

"The doctors and the detectives in the hospital questioned me about my dad," said Sarah R.

"They care about you," said the hot dog vendor.

"And they callously reminded me of my mother's death by ticketing me for scattering her ashes across the lake," she said.

"That's unfortunate," said the hot dog vendor, brushing away the grass that had left an imprint on her cheek.

"While I can't vouch for the sensitivity of doctors and detectives," he continued, "I hope I can convince you that hot dog vendors doubling as Dungeon Masters have better manners."

54. The Hot Dog Vendor

The man who was a hot dog vendor had, depending on one's point of view, multiple jobs, multiple personalities, or, as is the case with many a New Orleans native, multiple masques. Or, depending on one's point of view, the man possessed multiple all of the above.

Each job, or personality, or masque took an interest in Sarah R., but each had his own motives.

It was true. The hot dog vendor had kissed Sarah R. on the cheek after she was nearly struck by a speeding bus. He was a kind and simple man whose affectionate disposition crossed modern social boundaries. Yet, because of his noble countenance, no one ever protested. In fact, his bold but gentle gesture of affection toward Sarah R. came across as a refreshing and welcome anachronism.

This was why Sarah R. also did not protest when he slipped his business card in her cleavage. But the job, or personality, or masque who crossed that boundary was the Dungeon Master.

It was true. The Dungeon Master's motives, if not outright impure, were at best suspect. If he wasn't unethical, he was at least cynically self-interested. The Dungeon Master needed customers, especially young female customers, for his bar, and Sarah R. was eager to oblige the man's efforts to survive in this Hobbesian world.

It occurred to Sarah R. that the man probably had additional jobs, or personalities, or masques that he didn't reveal to her. But of this she was unconcerned. She understood it was best not to pry.

PART VIII

55. The Cracked Snail

Pellet of poison. Boot of orderly. Zachary's mower. Snail's soliloquy.

The Cracked Snail had committed itself to the asylum lawn long before Zachary R.'s arrival, when it learned it was the only snail who could communicate with humans.

The snail made this discovery one mad day as it was meandering among the blades thinking "Service to mankind," when from high above the boot of an orderly crashed down on its shell, cracking it and revealing its innards, which glistened in the searing mental sun. The snail screamed in pain and cursed at the orderly, who, to their mutual shock, heard the snail and went running for solitary confinement.

And so the Cracked Snail determined it would talk to the asylum patients, but would do so selectively so as not to worsen their already fragile psyches.

Years later, when Zachary R. was committed, the Cracked Snail took a keen interest in him due to his right-angle chin and his eyes, which blossomed like sunflowers. But the snail did not speak to him out of concern for his fragile psyche, which was confirmed beyond all doubt a month into his stay, when he first claimed to the snail that he had Neosporin. After all, no human in his right mind would offer Neosporin to a snail, crack or no crack.

But after a year in the asylum, Zachary R. said to someone important, "I like rivers and women." These words got him permission to mow the asylum lawn, much to the Cracked Snail's amusement and chagrin. The Cracked Snail's already keen interest in Zachary R. was heightened due to the intensity with which Zachary R. mowed the asylum lawn. The poison pellets did wonders to relieve the pain of the crack, but nevertheless the Cracked Snail had no desire to have its wound worsened by the blade of a lawn mower. And so the Cracked Snail kept extra vigilant watch over Zachary R. when Zachary mowed the asylum lawn.

On one such occasion, Zachary R. was mowing the asylum lawn, admiring the precision of grass, when he noticed a glint in the blades. He cut the engine and then stared for hours at the Cracked Snail, until finally Zachary R. again claimed, "I have Neosporin."

"Thanks," replied the Cracked Snail, "but you shouldn't use Neosporin on a wound of this magnitude. And, more importantly, as to your intense level of concentration in mowing the lawn, if you could spare some of that intensity for painting my portrait, I would like that very much."

Betraying neither shock nor horror at the fact of being spoken to by a snail, Zachary R. replied, "I don't know anything about painting."

"Don't be so modest," said the Cracked Snail.

56. The Lavender Bush and the Night Sky

Zachary R. wandered the perimeter of the asylum lawn in the searing mental sun. He stopped when he saw the Cracked Snail. He stared briefly and then proclaimed, "I'm lost."

The Cracked Snail replied, "Go to the corner and look into the lavender bush." Zachary R. went to the corner and looked into the lavender bush. He saw five bees. He continued to look into the lavender bush. He saw twenty bees. He continued to look into the lavender bush. He saw a hundred bees.

That night he sat up in bed, unbearably awake because of chess with his father. He thought about the bees in the lavender bush. He rose out of bed and went to the asylum window. He looked into the night sky. He saw a thousand stars. He continued to look into the night sky. He saw ten thousand stars. He continued to look into the night sky. He saw knights, rooks, and bishops.

57. Proselytize with Those Eyes

Zachary R. sat in the exact middle of the asylum lawn, thoroughly engrossed by the Cracked Snail as it slithered among the green blades in the searing mental sun.

Up the entire length of a blade it went, innards glistening, until the blade bent down for a soft landing, and then continuing along the dirt, stopping to nibble on a poison pellet, and back up another green blade until the blade bent down for another soft landing. All afternoon this continued, inducing a monk-like trance in Zachary R., whose eyes blossomed like sunflowers. Finally, the Cracked Snail stopped and, in a poison pellet-induced stupor, proclaimed, "You could proselytize with those eyes."

58. The Asylum Lawn

As depressed as an orderly, Zachary R. lay in the exact middle of the asylum lawn and imagined rows of pine trees in a pool of heat waves, the searing mental sun, the black sun of empathy, Annabel R., Sarah R., the Goth Girls, the Cracked Snail, shacks, cigarettes, chess, his father, his mother, the endless train, the Cold Angel, the flyswatter, the carnival, Bernrd Red, the lavender bush, and the night sky all beating down.

PART IX

59. News from the Working Parts, Part 1

A month out of the asylum, the foreclosure finalized, the boxcar journey complete, Zachary R. released himself to the soft prison of Hollywood in search of his daughter.

He cleared a spot for observation just off the Walk of Fame, on a stretch of pavement between medium buildings.

He gathered magazines, popped pills, worked a dainty jackhammer.

He wrote a suicide note on the back of a clipboard and sealed it in a business reply envelope.

He rolled up a *Newsweek* and a *Hustler*, and peered through them like binoculars. Unable to concentrate on the boulevard, he lifted his head to examine the sky, which was the same as examining the past. He saw knights, rooks, and bishops.

To his left was a beer bottle and a hat rack with a sailor's hat on it. He dropped the magazines and ignored the hat, but he uncapped and recapped the bottle several times, mimicking the working parts of Hollywood billboards.

He sampled his fingers: semen on the index, beer on the middle, stardom on the ring, asthma on the pinky, murder on the thumb. He turned and punched the building behind him. Pain traveled from his hand to his mind and back to his hand.

He looked at the boulevard. There was no sign of his daughter. He watched the megaphone arm of a police car cock and then heard the words, "Driver of the blue truck, get out of the way." He heard the blue truck ram the car in front of it and the ensuing siren.

He watched girls mine for teeth jewels and boys fake gayness for the sake of slavery, but really they all missed trick-or-treating with foster parents.

Zachary R. took notice of the boys because the boys had caught a glimpse of his right-angle chin and the dainty jackhammer, which no longer worked due to the pain in his hand. Nevertheless, the boys pushed up their sleeves, pursed their lips, and moved toward him. Zachary R. leapt to his feet and bull-rushed them, believing their flirtation would wither in his malodor. He was correct. The boys ushered him along, shirts raised to cover their noses.

He continued walking until he came upon a corpse at the base of the hills by the youth hostel. Searchlights crossed overhead. He heard Haydn. A soft breeze moved his arm hairs. His hand began to swell. He reached for the lifeless body and said, "I am afraid to die."

60. Wind in Empty Boxes

Woodward and Bernstein. Bonnie and Clyde. Heckle and Jeckle. Jekyll and Hyde.

Morning came and Zachary R. was back on his stretch of pavement between medium buildings. Eyes were all around him: vendors and vice, bankers and bondsmen, and two newsmen questioning a male and a female detective about a corpse found by the youth hostel near the Hollywood Bowl.

Zachary R. did his best to look tilted and full of space. He sampled the fingers on his injured hand, which was now swollen to the point of immobility.

He was unbearably awake and black with hunger.

He zipped his pants and put on the sailor's hat. He thought about the night before, about Haydn and the corpse, and about his time in the asylum when he fought Bernrd Red over the Electric Light Dirge for Cello and Organ.

He boarded the bus to Santa Monica and sat directly behind the driver, who smelled like wind in empty boxes.

In Santa Monica, Zachary R. walked in the wet sand. Gulls and pigeons made him duck and weave to the delight of Goth Girls, who had frenzied the birds to conjure storms from the ocean. He bull-rushed them and said in a mock English accent, "You have a spectacular arsenal of spells." The girls raised their Damien lockets to cover their giggling faces and vanished in the ocean air.

He turned and walked to the pier with the endless carnival. He ordered a beer and a banana and watched the grand wheel until the sun went down. Then he went to the edge of the pier and watched the waves.

He dove in just as it began to rain, expecting the current to carry him to shore. But just the opposite happened. He drifted out to sea, past the continental shelf and into a vast fishing net that scooped him aboard a Yin Yang liner bound for all ports south around Cape Horn and then north to Rio and the Caribbean, with a final destination of New Orleans, where a ramp was extended and he disembarked.

Zachary R. woke along the shore of Venice Beach, coughing up ocean. He wished for a possibility other than life or death.

61. Dumbfounded as a Refugee

Zachary R. stood on the sand of Venice Beach, dumbfounded as a refugee. He took three steps east and fell face-first onto a mound of seaweed, causing a splash of flies that attached en masse to his body.

He rolled like he was on fire, rolled until the flies had flown or were smashed, rolled until the bananas and the beer from the night before reemerged in his mouth mixed with bile. He spit out the entire apparatus, which diminished his vertigo. He stood again, free of entanglements.

He scraped his salty wet clothes with a stick, and set off on foot toward the hill of shacks and cigarettes. He walked for eight miles, recalling the joy of nails in his lips and the comfort of flowing blood.

By evening he had returned to his stretch of pavement between medium buildings.

He felt in his pockets for burger money but found only sand and tar.

He turned gray and curled up where pavement and building met, where the warmth of the day had been retained.

Three Goth Girls surrounded him to block the chill, but this did little to prevent the ensuing fever and the further blackening of his injured hand. Puzzled, the girls painted their nails white and prayed.

62. The Street Boys and the Dainty Jackhammer

After all he had been through in the soft prison of Hollywood—his injured hand, the corpse, the bus ride to the ocean and diving off the pier and being washed ashore and coughing up ocean, the flies on the beach and rolling in the sand like he was on fire, the long walk back to Hollywood, back to his stretch of pavement between medium buildings with no burger money and fever and the further blackening of his injured hand—Zachary R. had forgotten about the boys who fake gayness for the sake of slavery, the street boys, but the boys did not forget Zachary R.

The boys had taken notice of Zachary R.'s right-angle chin, and they hadn't forgotten the glimpse of the dainty jackhammer and how he made them wither in his malodor.

So the boys kept an eye on the alley and waited for Zachary R.'s return. When he returned from his bus ride to the ocean, the boys pushed up their sleeves, pursed their lips, and moved toward him.

There were three street boys in all and Zachary R. was in no condition to bull-rush them this time. The defense of his malodor, the dark-road signature of the skunk, had been diminished by the sea.

The first boy spoke: "If it isn't the bum with the pretty chin and the dainty jackhammer."

Then the second boy: "And he smells pretty, too, like the ocean and not like a skunk. Much better." He took a deep whiff.

And then the third boy: "He does smell better. Must be trying to impress us this time. Let's see that chin smile. Let's have a look at that dainty jackhammer."

All three boys laughed loudly. The third boy shoved him to the ground.

Zachary R. turned gray. He covered his ears with his hands and moved his knees to his chest.

The third boy yanked Zachary R. by the arm with such force that he went from lying down to sitting up straight.

Zachary R. grimaced in pain.

"No smile from that pretty chin?" the first boy taunted. "No glimpse of that dainty jackhammer?"

Zachary R. grimaced again, giggled terribly, and said, "I'm neither gay nor gay, so I guess the three of you little cocksuckers will just have to fuck yourselves tonight."

The only memory Zachary R. retained from this night was the sound of what seemed like every trashcan in the alley crashing down on him and the laughter of the street boys, which sounded like crows and made him see sunspots.

63. Puke, Porn, and a Pit Bull

Street boys, crows, and sunspots. Zachary R., all slender and milky, thought dark thoughts as he dragged himself along his stretch of pavement. He cursed God over his committal, which separated him from daughter and home.

"Just let me die here in peace," he pled.

His plea was not granted. A murder of crows shrieked above, while all around him hovered puke, porn, and a pit bull.

But God did not ignore him altogether: That bald family man good-vibed him with a thunderclap that startled the pit bull and sent it into a cardboard box.

That night it rained cold and hard. Water ran down the sides of buildings and down the hills. Water joined puke and disappeared into a storm drain. Water saturated porn and bled colors into pavement.

The morning sun revealed a new city, like the beginning of ancient ruins. Zachary R. hummed

Haydn. He thought fondly of the Electric Light Dirge for Cello and Organ. The swelling in his hand seemed to recede.

64. The Wheels of a Trashcan

The wheels of a trashcan rolled slowly over Zachary R.'s stretch of pavement between medium buildings, crunching and popping gravel, and causing his neck to tingle with delight.

Memories of carnival straw and smoke.

Thoughts of Annabel.

"Why do the police whisper all the time?" he thought.

"Why are they always looking at me?"

Thoughts of Sarah.

"Where could she be?" he said out loud.

Zachary R. reached inside the trashcan and pulled out a large brown bag.

Inside the bag were a hamburger and a bathrobe. He bit into the burger, but it tasted of worms, microbes, and malodor. He tried on the bathrobe, but it smelled like Ben Gay.

65. Like a Ghost Ship

A bus stopped near Zachary R.'s stretch of pavement between medium buildings in the early morning hours. The inside of the bus was dark, like a ghost ship. The electric letters that moved along the top read, "NOT IN SERVICE."

The driver swung open the door and stepped outside for a cigarette.

The boulevard was quiet.

Zachary R. approached the driver. His injured hand began to throb.

"Where does this bus go?" he asked.

"Around the perimeter," said the driver.

"Can I go with you?"

"No."

"Why did you stop here, then?"

"To smoke a cigarette."

"Have you seen my daughter?"

"Yes. And your wife, too. They're looking for you."

66. The Goth Girls and the Ghost Ship

Seven Goth Girls filed out the side door of the bus and descended with great conviction upon Zachary R., who was still harassing the bus driver on his cigarette break.

"Why do you think he said he was going around the perimeter?" they asked in unison. "He was afraid of what you might do to him if he told you the truth.

"The truth is that your mother and wife are dead, and your daughter is in New Orleans.

"The truth is that your daughter tricked you into coming to L.A. because she is afraid and ashamed of you.

"The truth is that you are going around the perimeter of the truth by living in this alley and acting crazy.

"The truth is that you are not responsible for your mother's death, but you are responsible for Annabel's death, though only partially. Her death was largely her own fault and that of her other lover, Bernrd Red."

"That's enough truth for now," said Zachary R.

He felt ill and at peace simultaneously.

The redheaded Goth approached him and held his injured hand.

67. The Arrest

It looked like Easter clouds on the morning of Zachary R.'s arrest for the murder of H. James Branhoover of Pittsburgh, Pennsylvania.

Though his name had a princely air, Mr. Branhoover was, in fact, a runaway living in a youth hostel on Highland Avenue, just south of the Hollywood Bowl.

Mr. Branhoover had either fallen to his death from the roof of the youth hostel, or he had been pushed. No suicide note had been found, there were fingerprints on his clothes, and one eyewitness, a gay male prostitute, said he saw a homeless man reaching for the body and muttering, "I am afraid to die."

Zachary R. sat alone in a holding cell, watching sunlight shine through the lone barred window and move across the floor as the hours passed by.

Finally, two detectives, one male and one female, entered and escorted Zachary R. to an interrogation room for questioning.

It didn't take expert detective work to determine that Zachary R. had nothing to do with the death of H. James Branhoover, or to determine that Zachary R. was in need of medical attention for his injured hand and for his broken mind and desolate spirit.

It would have taken expert detective work, however, or even clairvoyance, to uncover the unlikely connection between Zachary R. and H. James Branhoover. Fortunately for Zachary R., the detectives did not possess such powers.

Zachary R. told the detectives about his daughter, his mother, the Cold Angel, boxcars, subways and endless trains, his father and chess, his wife and Bernrd Red, his pleasant conversations with the Cracked Snail, the peace of mowing the asylum lawn, and the tormenting and nurturing Goth Girls.

The detectives were good listeners, but their logical minds were incapable of comprehending Zachary R.'s story. At least they got him to a hospital to get his injured hand looked at.

As for H. James Branhoover, a suicide note was eventually found. He had sealed and mailed it in a business reply envelope for *Playboy* magazine.

The ladies at the subscription processing center in Boulder, Colorado were moved by the poignant words and the urgent message contained in Mr. Branhoover's note. In fact, one of the ladies photocopied the note and shared it with her son, who had run away twice before.

The note dispelled romantic notions of the lives of runaways and demonstrated just how ugly Hollywood really is. The lady's son never ran away again. Instead, he waited until he turned eighteen and then he moved to Las Cruces, New Mexico, where he got a job, found a wife, went back to school, and eventually became a professor

in the Humanities Department of New Mexico
State University.

68. Worms, Microbes, Malodor

Zachary R.'s hand was put in a cast at the
hospital, but the doctor there was less concerned
about the broken hand than he was about the
infection that had begun to spread.

The doctor, realizing that Zachary R. was
homeless, was determined not to let him take the
bed of an insured patient, but he wasn't totally
devoid of pity. He had asked enough questions
during intake to determine that Zachary R. had
been previously placed in an asylum in
Massachusetts, and he attempted to devise a way
for Zachary R. to be committed to a comparable
facility in California.

The doctor knew that Zachary R. was in need of intravenous antibiotics for the infection in his injured hand, which had begun to move up his arm en route to his brain. He also knew, however, that he needed to process Zachary R. as quickly as possible in order to bring in the next—insured—patient.

A redheaded nurse with black lipstick and white painted fingernails brought Zachary R. a bottle of antibiotics and told him to return in a week for follow-up and for possible admission to the state hospital—the asylum—for his broken mind and desolate spirit.

Zachary R. explained that he found the asylum in Massachusetts to his liking as he was escorted out of the hospital in a wheelchair and deposited back into the soft prison of Hollywood.

He set the bottle of pills in a flowerbed and forgot about them as he made his way back to his stretch of pavement between medium buildings, his mind on knights, rooks, and bishops.

That night he felt a deep chill course through his body as the infection moved closer to his brain.

PART X

69. A Penny for Your Two Cents

Zachary R. knew his marriage was a mistake, but he naively hoped the wedding ritual would instill in Annabel R. a modicum of love— or at least respect or sentimentality.

But this was not the case. Annabel R. was a day tripper despite all the promise of the Mostly Silent matchbook slipped under Zachary R.'s door and their day at the carnival. Bernrd Red, the bed-and-breakfast concierge, understood this immediately when he saw Annabel R. at check-in on the first day of her honeymoon with Zachary R. Whenever possible, Bernrd Red would promote the sensation of being hit in the head with a rock by stealing the services of unscrupulous brides.

When Bernrd Red laid eyes on Annabel R. at the concierge desk, he could see that she would be an easy conquest. He fiddled with his pinky ring under the desk.

When Annabel R. laid eyes on Bernrd Red, the concierge, she could see that he would be a willing participant in her cigar box ritual. She began to sweat.

Annabel R. asked Zachary R. to inquire about the nineteenth-century bicycles at the rental shop across the street.

Zachary R. went gallantly, chivalrously, to do so. "The wedding has softened her," he thought.

When Zachary R. was out of earshot, Bernrd Red sneered at Annabel R. and said, "A penny for your two cents."

Without hesitation, Annabel R. told him her thoughts and invited Bernrd Red to meet her in the honeymoon suite just as soon as she could send her new husband on another errand.

She flashed the contents of the cigar box at Bernrd Red. A pair of brass knuckles. A romance novel called *Savage Splendor*.

Bernrd Red chuckled and handed her one of two keys to the honeymoon suite. He kept the other key for himself.

As Annabel R. was preparing the honeymoon suite for her paramour, there was a knock on the door.

She opened it fearfully, not knowing whose face would appear. It was Zachary R.'s face. He was holding brochures and maps of local hiking trails.

"The giant bicycles aren't for tourists," he said. "Only the staff are allowed to ride them."

"Of course," said Annabel R.

"I got some maps of hiking trails," said Zachary R.

"That's sweet of you," she said. "Would you mind going hiking without me today? I became ill while you were out. Pregnancy is getting to me."

Zachary R. obliged her, but he forgot to ask about a key to the room.

Some time later, Bernrd Red called the room and Annabel R. answered, confirming that she was alone and that her husband was off hiking for the afternoon.

The ritual beating began from the moment Bernrd Red walked through the door. Bernrd Red required no instruction from Annabel R. as to what to do, which frenzied her and made her whirl and pop.

Love came and went, and came and went again.

Zachary R., meanwhile, had gone no more than a mile down the road when it occurred to him that he didn't have a key to the honeymoon suite.

He felt the most considerate thing to do would be to return to the room at once, before his pregnant wife fell asleep. He made only one stop on his way back, to get pink bismuth for her stomach.

Zachary R. was several paces from the door when he heard the familiar sound of brass knuckles on flesh, as well as the whirling and popping.

He dropped to his knees and grabbed his haunches. Then, in a moment of terrible clarity and calm, he walked back down the hallway, out the door of the bed-and-breakfast, and into the mountains, where he hiked the longest trail on the map.

But before he turned the other cheek and walked away into the mountains, he turned around and looked in the window of the honeymoon suite, where he saw on the nightstand the glint of a ruby ring and a concierge badge with the name Bernrd Red written on it. Worse than these, he saw the grinning chin and the angry eyes of Bernrd Red. They would haunt him forever.

70. Wind Chimes and Lavender

Zachary R. woke to the face of his cheating wife, their heads on pillows in the honeymoon suite of a bed-and-breakfast on a road called Bath in a seaside village out West.

He turned away and opened a window. On the windowsill, silk roses and a ceramic dove.

He looked outside. In the courtyard couples whispered among wind chimes and lavender. On the sidewalk nineteenth-century bicycles went by, giant wheels in front, miniature wheels in back.

He grabbed his haunches and moved his knees to his chest.

His wife woke, said "Quit it," got dressed, rubbed a drop of rain on her neck, and went surfing alone. In the South, buildings and lungs collapsed.

Zachary R. turned gray. He pulled on his jeans and staggered shirtless up the road to a park, where he collapsed and curled up in the grass. A young Goth Girl with red hair and black lips knelt beside him, placed her hand on his shoulder, removed her coat, and covered him.

In the East, silver clouds enveloped the New Hampshire mountains.

In the New Hampshire mountains, a traveler pulled to the side of the road.

71. A Penny for Your Thoughts

On the third and final day of their honeymoon, Annabel R. woke to an empty bed. Remorse coursed through her bruised, concussed, scraped, and startled body. Why had her husband not returned? Could he know about Bernrd Red, the concierge? How could he? He didn't have a key to the room. He isn't waiting outside the door, is he?

Annabel R. slowly rolled out of bed, put on baggy warm-ups to hide the bruises on her pregnant body, and gently opened the door of the honeymoon suite. Zachary R. was not there.

Annabel R. felt relieved, but only for a moment, as relief was replaced by fear for what might have happened to him.

She went back inside for her sandals. Then she set off on foot up Bath Road until she found her husband lying in a park covered by a heavy black coat that was not his own.

Annabel R. knelt beside him, placed her hand on his shoulder, removed the heavy black coat, and stroked his hair until he woke.

He stared at her until the memory of who she was returned. "You smell like rain," he said.

"Yes, I know," said Annabel R. "It's the scent of the perfume I wear."

Suddenly Zachary R. began to recall the events from the two previous days. He saw the face of Bernrd Red. The sunflowers in his eyes wilted.

Annabel R. stroked his face with her fingers and said, "A penny for your thoughts."

"I want to go home," said Zachary R. "What time is the flight?"

72. Pregnant Pause

The post-honeymoon flight home was quiet and tense for Zachary R. and Annabel R. and for the baby in Annabel R.'s womb. The baby kicked and squirmed in unison with the turbulence at thirty-five-thousand feet.

Zachary R. obsessed on the moment of betrayal. His angry thoughts came through loudly to Annabel R., even though his actions spoke of a happy newlywed with a child on the way.

He rubbed his wife's expanding belly, and he held her hand and spoke gently and lovingly and dutifully. He convinced himself that it was all genuine, but his wife and everyone else onboard the flight could feel the rumbling volcano in seat 26A.

So Zachary R. and Annabel R. each had a secret. He withheld having witnessed his wife with Bernrd Red, and she withheld having had the affair with Bernrd Red and at least one other man.

And while there was very little that was genuine in their marriage, there was the overriding fact of their forthcoming daughter, who kept them together.

During the final trimester of Annabel's pregnancy, Zachary R. and Annabel R. continued to live in their separate apartments in the building with the hall with the blue carpet.

And then Sarah R. was born, and the family of three moved into the house where Sarah R. would one day drive the Nova through the living room window.

73. Dutiful Zachary

Dutiful Zachary pushed down his grief and relief that his wife was dead, pushed them down next to his mother in her tissue-fiber nightgown and his chess-obsessed father, pushed them down next to Bernrd Red, who greeted Annabel R. with a rueful smile and read passages from *Savage Splendor*, as if the ritual belonged to them and not to her and Zachary. Bernrd Red, to whom Zachary R. had never uttered a word except in his capacity as concierge of the bed-and-breakfast, but whom—if not for the fact that it would have jeopardized his chances for Messiah or Rock Star—he gladly would have murdered in any number of grisly ways.

Dutiful Zachary indulged the violent fantasy of his righteous murder of Bernrd Red. The fantasy always a sharp axe and a tilted stare with varying methods of delivery, and always the same witness, Annabel R.

And then he pushed down this fantasy to greet a snickering Bernrd Red and a snarling Annabel R., who mocked Zachary R. with the words, "I'm already dead, but you never could have gone through with it anyway. You were a harmless nobody with your wilting sunflower eyes. Everybody could see what you were up to. You're no saint. You're a deluded coward who didn't even have the guts to put a stop to his own cheating wife on their own honeymoon."

Dutiful Zachary pushed down his dead wife. "Sharp axes are for pine trees and leisure," he muttered. "Hold onto your job and raise your daughter," he said to himself.

And these thoughts were pure and these thoughts were righteous, but Zachary R. neglected his grief, and his grief became shame and his shame became anger and his grief, shame, and anger festered like worms, microbes, and malodor.

* * * * *

Sarah R. thought her father was a bit uptight because of his obsession with mowing the lawn, but otherwise she felt safe and content and taken care of during her first fourteen years.

Had she known what he was battling inside, she would have identified his struggle as a Hobbesian choice, a dilemma.

Zachary R. could have confronted Bernrd Red and the pregnant Annabel R. in the honeymoon suite, but that would have had only one possible outcome: a violent struggle that would certainly have resulted in serious injury or death to one, two, or all three involved . . . all four if the in utero Sarah R. was included.

His alternative, which, of course, was what he chose to do, was to turn the other cheek and allow the events in the honeymoon suite that day to run their course. He would push down the pain for the sake of peace that day and peace for the future of the marriage and the baby.

Zachary R. hoped that his wife would outgrow her taste for brass knuckles and romance novels and that there was a possibility for some kind of normalcy in the future.

But Annabel R. gave birth to Sarah R. and a week later she was arranging trysts not only with Bernrd Red—who visited Boston as frequently as he could, expensing flights for "concierge conventions" or anything related or not to the hospitality industry, so long as it brought him to the bedroom of Annabel R.—but also with the gardener who gardened the neighbor's house across the street every Tuesday at eleven o'clock, when Zachary R. was hard at work at Miller & Associates and Sarah R. was in her crib.

But with the ever-increasing frequency and duration of the trysts came increased trips to the emergency room to care for her injuries.

Because there was no attributing her injuries to anything but brass knuckles, the doctors and nurses at the hospital began to suspect Zachary R. of spousal abuse. Eventually, though, Annabel R., to keep her affairs a secret, was forced to admit them to the doctors and nurses.

She was forced to admit that the beatings came at her own request and that her husband was not to blame, that he used to indulge her fetish but now refused. She was forced to make this confession or risked losing her baby, her two paramours, and her cuckold husband, who remained dutiful and true for her sake and the baby's sake and also for the sake of keeping alive his chances for Messiah or Rock Star.

The doctors and nurses warned Annabel R. of the dangers of blunt trauma to the head and other areas of her body, as well as of the seriousness of multiple concussions. They officially attributed her fetish to postpartum depression and, like Zachary R., hoped it was all a passing phase.

* * * * *

Annabel R. must have known her days were numbered, because her behavior began to change. She began to dote on her baby, reading passages from "The Little Match Girl" to Sarah R. in her crib. She began to call off visits from her paramours. After two such postponements, and because he began to hear nothing but the voices of Crosby, Stills, Nash & Young singing "Carry On," Bernrd Red checked himself into the asylum. Upon discharge, he never set foot in Boston again. As for the gardener, he kept right on gardening at the neighbor's house across the street.

Annabel R. even began to take Sarah R. around the block in a squeaky pram that Zachary R. deliberately failed to oil because the sound of the squeaky wheel signified the rehabilitation of his wife and the possibility of happiness.

Zachary R. was beginning to feel vindicated in his decision to remain passive throughout the ordeal, until the morning when Annabel R. failed to wake up.

The autopsy revealed that Annabel R. had died of a brain hemorrhage brought on by chronic blunt trauma to the head.

Dutiful Zachary pushed down his grief and relief that she was gone. He had Annabel R.

cremated and her ashes placed in an urn. He hired a nanny to care for his two-year-old daughter. He continued to go to work every morning at the Law Offices of Miller & Associates.

Dutiful Zachary oiled the squeaky wheel on the pram, which the nanny pushed along the sidewalk in silence.

74. Your Story Is My Story

Zachary R. lay in bed in the asylum, feeling lonely as an aisle of concrete in the moonlight, feeling well. Bernrd Red burst through the door, bull-rushed the bed, and yelled, "My story is your story!"

Zachary R. grabbed a paperweight off the nightstand and threw it at Bernrd Red.

It missed by a wide margin. Both men were relieved.

Zachary R. apologized.

"No," said Bernrd Red. "I understand. What I meant to say is your story is my story."

Zachary R. felt the sensation of being hit in the head with a rock. He lunged for Bernrd Red, but Bernrd Red grabbed him and wrestled him to the floor. When Bernrd Red had Zachary R. pinned, he sneered, and said, "You're more like me than you think. You despise me for beating and sleeping with your wife, for betraying you. You had an infuriating innocence that made me want to hurt you. You betrayed a man you didn't know when you took Annabel to the carnival and knocked her up. I'll bet you didn't know that, did you? She told me all about it and we laughed at your ignorant self-righteousness."

"Whatever," mumbled Zachary R.

75. Bernrd Red Finds the Accommodations in the Alley Disagreeable

Zachary R. sat on his stretch of pavement between medium buildings nursing his injured hand and humming Haydn when from off the Walk of Fame came Bernrd Red.

Bernrd Red despised music. He looked down the alley and locked eyes with Zachary R. He covered his ears and glared as he headed down the alley to menace him.

"Long time no see," said Bernrd Red. "What brings you to a Hollywood alley?"

As he continued his approach, Zachary R.'s malodor thickened and Bernrd Red was forced to move his hands from his ears to his shirt, which he raised to cover his nose.

Zachary R. was preparing in his mind to explain about searching for his daughter when he noticed Bernrd Red's displeasure.

"What's the matter?" asked Zachary R. "Do you find my new accommodations less agreeable than the asylum?"

"You reek!" exclaimed Bernrd Red through his shirt, turning and walking purposefully back toward the Walk of Fame.

"And stay away!" shouted Zachary R., giggling terribly.

And Bernrd Red did stay away; in fact, he never visited Zachary R. again.

PART XI

76. Skyscraper File Clerk

In the twenty years between high school and his committal, Zachary R. worked as a file clerk in the file storage room of the Law Offices of Miller & Associates.

Miller & Associates was a large firm that had been around since Teddy Roosevelt was president. As a result of its size and age, and because of the firm's conservative document retention policy, the file storage room occupied the entire top floor of the fourth-largest skyscraper in Boston.

Zachary R. was one of three file clerks, but due to the private nature of file clerks, there was little or no interaction among them. The floor was quiet except for the sound of shuffling papers. There were no human sounds or even machine sounds, as the photocopier was in the litigation department on the floor below.

Miller & Associates' files were arranged using a twelve-digit sequence of numbers and no color coding.

Numbers, papers, and photocopies. This was how Zachary R. earned a wage.

There was no need for thought since only patterns of numbers occupied his mind. There was a lot of room, therefore, for daydreams and fantasies at the photocopier downstairs. The sound of the photocopier and of others working their machines scintillated his brain: Keyboards clicking. Phones ringing. The mechanics of a bustling office. Graves being dug in the continents of the world.

When he went downstairs to make photocopies, it was as if he had entered the vibrant City of Letters after years in exile in the stagnant City of Numbers, unable to speak or understand the world of words. The numbers had stolen his identity.

77. International Harvester of Souls

One day, during the days and nights leading up to his committal, Zachary R. arrived at Miller & Associates lit by the black sun of empathy. His mind was on numbers, as usual, until he went downstairs to make copies.

Keyboards clicking. Phones ringing. Graves being dug in the continents of the world.

The Red Cross nurse appeared. She removed her nun's habit. She was the Cold Angel.

The Cold Angel ran her veil over his scalp and said, "Isn't it time you quit this job? Isn't it time to save the world? Isn't it time to atone for the deaths of your mother and your wife?"

Zachary R. stared at the wrinkles around her eyes and proclaimed, "International harvester of souls."

He left the papers in the photocopier, took the elevator down to the ground floor, and vowed never to set foot in Miller & Associates again.

78. Shacks and Cigarettes

Zachary R. walked out the front door of Miller & Associates and set off on foot toward the New Hampshire mountains, saying, "Service to Mankind, Service to Mankind."

With his mind no longer occupied by numbers, Zachary R. lost his bearings. He disconnected. He genuinely believed he was on a mission, but friends, family, and bystanders could plainly see that he was disintegrating.

He went into a hardware store for supplies for his mission, which was shacks and cigarettes for all, roofs over their heads and smoke in their lungs, train after train with boxcars full of smoke and lumber, saving the world like a Messiah or Rock Star.

But if there were to be smoke and lumber, there also needed to be nails to bring it all together.

Zachary R. walked down the aisle of the hardware store and reached into a barrel of nails that rattled and brushed his spine like silk, urging him to nap.

He lay down on an aisle of concrete in the outdoor nursery and slept until the store opened the next morning.

Security shook him awake and ushered him out the door.

Job was lost. Wife was cremated. Pram did not squeak.

But Zachary R. still believed in the morning.

He determined that he would need a heavy coat for his trip into the New Hampshire mountains. He found one in an abandoned shed along the riverbank. He reached into the pockets and found a burger and a pack of cigarettes. "This was somebody's home," he thought.

He bit into the burger: worms, microbes, malodor. He threw it down in disgust.

He lit a cigarette. Carnival smoke. Brown earth smoke. Gypsy kids. He flicked the cigarette onto the hard dirt floor of the shed and watched it smolder.

It was late afternoon when Zachary R. felt he should get home to tell his daughter about quitting his job and about departing on his mission.

He fell asleep in the shed while wearing the heavy coat. He dreamt about his mother in her tissue-fiber nightgown and about the parrot out of its cage shitting on the kitchen stove.

Zachary R. didn't make it home that night. Instead, he left the shed and walked south along the river and its tributaries, thinking "I like rivers and women" instead of "Service to mankind," which was what he meant to think.

Now he was confused. He felt ill. The burger had made him sick. He stumbled along the riverbank and vomited violently. The burger was bad. He became feverish. He hummed Haydn. He thought about where he might have been in the years before his birth. He vomited some more. He decided he had better get home to Sarah.

79. Evil Men

Zachary R. and Sarah R. lived in a twilit bungalow on the outskirts of Boston, in a town with a cemetery dating to a time before the Revolutionary War.

The town was quiet and the neighbors were easily woken, which presented a problem for Zachary R. when he discovered that he had lost his keys somewhere between work, the shed, and vomiting up the bad burger.

He circled the perimeter of the house quietly and tested windows to try to break into without disturbing his daughter. They were all shut tight. Then he arrived at the front door and turned the knob, which, to his chagrin and delight, had been left unlocked.

Sarah R. was sitting on the sofa waiting for him.

"Sarah, why are you still up? It must be way past your bedtime," said Zachary R.

"It's only eight o'clock," said Sarah R., unnerved at the sight of her father.

"Why are you wearing that ratty overcoat?" she asked. "It smells. Are you all right? You're pale and you smell like puke. Dad, what's happening? You're scaring me."

"My mom wore a ratty tissue-fiber nightgown and we had a parrot out of its cage that shit on the kitchen stove and all my dad cared about was chess," said Zachary R.

"We lived in a twilit bungalow like this one, but your mom and I agreed this one would be clean. No parrot. No grease stains on the driveway, no sunflowers painted thick on the mailbox, no chess," he said, all lit up by the searing mental sun.

Zachary R. took the urn with Annabel R.'s ashes down from the mantel and explained: "Your mom allowed evil men like her father, and another man I won't even mention, to corrupt her.

"I thought that if I could love her long enough, she would allow her better side to prevail. But in the end, her cheating and her concussions did her in.

"Did you know your mom liked Hans Christian Andersen, Sarah?"

"Dad, what are you talking about!? You never told me Mom cheated on you. You're scaring me. Why are your work clothes so dirty? Why do you smell like puke? There *are* grease stains on the driveway. The Nova has been leaking for years. There's no such thing as a tissue-fiber nightgown. There *are* no parrots. Have you lost your mind?!"

Zachary R. was nonplussed. He wiped his brow. "How old are you, Sarah? Thirteen?"

"No, fourteen. C'mon."

"It's time for you to learn how to drive. It's time for you to start giving. Time to start donating blood. If you don't start behaving, you're going to wind up like your mother."

"Dad, did you quit your job?" asked Sarah R.

"Yes, I did," said Zachary R., now completely deflated.

"Then how are you going to pay the bills?" she asked, meekly, starting to cry. "If we get evicted, then you're the evil one."

The sunflowers in his eyes wilted, but he wasn't going back to Miller & Associates. It was too late. It was too late for work. It was too late for raising a daughter. It was too late for living in a home with a roof over his head. It was too late for Zachary R.

Zachary R. handed Sarah R. the urn. She opened it and stared at the ashes, searching for humanity. She closed the urn and set it back on the mantel. Then she turned and looked hopelessly at her father.

"Can you forgive me?" Zachary R. asked.

80. Aisle of Concrete in the Moonlight

Zachary R. woke earlier than he expected to the next morning because he wasn't done getting sick. He stumbled past Sarah's bedroom and into the bathroom, where he dry heaved three painful dry heaves. There was no bad burger left in his stomach to heave up. He drank water out of the bathroom faucet, and then he reached for the flyswatter by the toilet and recited these words:

"Forehand, backhand, microphone, guitar, spider on shoulder, cockroach on soap bar slipping, slipping, slipping."

A fourth dry heave ensued, but it was a little less painful because of the water. Sarah R. cracked open the bathroom door and saw her father lying on the cold tile still in the heavy coat, knees pulled tight to his chest, and clutching the flyswatter.

"Are you going to be okay, Dad? Should I call 911?" she asked.

"I'm almost better," said Zachary R. "Please don't call 911, I'll be okay in a minute. Go back to bed."

Sarah R. shut the bathroom door. Zachary R. could hear her footsteps heading back to her bedroom. He felt ill again, but not from the bad burger; rather, he felt ill from shame and doubt and fear. He needed to expedite the mission.

Zachary R. rose from the bathroom tile, buttoned his heavy coat, and set off on foot toward the abandoned shed along the riverbank to retrieve the nails and cigarettes that would build a smoking, smoldering habitat for humanity.

When he arrived at the shed, he recalled that he had no nails, lumber, or otherwise for the construction of his worldwide shacks. All he found on the hard dirt floor of the shed was an open pack of cigarettes, one half-smoked cigarette butt, and the remainder of the bad burger, which had decayed almost beyond recognition.

He would need to return to the hardware store to procure supplies.

Zachary R. walked along the riverbank, thinking about rivers and women instead of service to mankind.

He considered the definition of insanity: "to do the same thing over and over and expect different results." He went to the bar anyway.

Zachary R. stumbled among the barstools and pool tables, blurting out, "Cigar boxes and romance novels are the brass knuckles of sex" to anyone who would listen, which was no one, except for the bartender, who kindly offered to pour Zachary R. a complimentary Wild Turkey if Zachary would kindly sit down and leave the paying customers alone.

Zachary R. managed to finagle five drinks for the price of none. He exited out the back, stinking of bourbon, and with a heightened urgency to get on with his mission. He set off on foot to the hardware store to pick up supplies, but by the time he arrived, night had fallen and the store was closed.

He picked up a substantial stone, expecting he would need to bust a window to get inside. To his great relief, however, the door had been left unlocked.

He entered the hardware store and began gathering supplies in a shopping cart: screws and lumber, saws and hammers, levels and pencils.

But then he reached into the barrel of nails that rattled and brushed his spine like silk and urged him to nap.

Zachary R. left the cart behind and made his way to the outdoor nursery, where he lay down on an aisle of concrete.

The Cold Angel knelt down beside him, rubbed his back like winter, and asked, "Are you lonely as the cello?"

"No," said Zachary R. "I am lonely as an aisle of concrete in the moonlight."

81. A Peculiar Shade of Burgundy, Part 2

Sarah R. understood that her father was descending into madness and that she had better figure out a few things about surviving as a fourteen-year-old adult.

She would have to mooch. She would have to learn to drive the Nova. She would have to act at school like nothing was wrong. She would have to do what her father asked and give blood. Maybe she could find a part-time job at the Red Cross. Maybe she could learn to gamble or prostitute herself. Maybe she could become a hitman at school, injecting arsenic into teachers' apples.

What she was most concerned about, though, was guarding the urn with her mother's ashes. With her father no longer able to support her, she gained an appreciation, even an obsession, with the sanctity of death, which she now understood to be the ultimate fact of life.

* * * * *

On the other hand, with her father away on his mission, Sarah R. felt encouraged to do some exploration of her own. She decided to ditch school one morning and take an inventory of the house. She surveyed the main rooms and the garage, which held no major surprises, save for a stack of orange cones, which she hadn't noticed before.

Then she went through the closets and found nothing of interest until she arrived at the closet in the master bedroom, which she knew had an opening in the ceiling that led into the attic.

The first thing she noticed about the attic was that it was warmer than the rest of the house.

The next thing she noticed was a trunk that contained her parents' things.

- Carnival items: a small poster ad with illustrations of trapeze artists and elephants; stuffed animals; a roll of unused tickets.

- A copy of Hans Christian Andersen's *Fairy Tales* with a bookmark at the story called "The Little Match Girl."

- A photo of Zachary R.'s parents, whom Annabel R. never met, his father sitting at the dining room table surveying a chessboard; his mother, looking tired and daft in her tissue-fiber nightgown; a parrot perched on the back of a chair.

- A cigar box with a pair of brass knuckles, a romance novel called *Savage Splendor*, and a CD called Electric Light Dirge for Cello and Organ.

At the bottom of the trunk was a dress in a peculiar shade of burgundy with the word *Revolution* written on the tag inside, where the washing instructions would normally be.

Sarah R. tried on the Revolution Dress, which must have been her mother's, because the word *Revolution* was written in her mother's hand. The dress made Sarah R. burn with weakness. She felt reckless and charitable. She suddenly knew how she would survive without her father, as, essentially, an orphan.

It would be blood drives and blackjack, kittens and heroin, apples and arsenic, and trick-or-treating with foster parents.

82. A Peculiar Shade of Burgundy, Part 1

Insurrection was in the thrift store air when a peculiar shade of burgundy caught the corner of Annabel R.'s eye. She paid the three dollars to the fop behind the counter and she wore the dress out the door and onto the street, where she promptly became aware that her secondhand dress possessed first-rate power.

The dress compelled her feet to walk in a new way and her insides to burn with a strange and powerful weakness. Her burning insides and her new walking feet led her into a scent shop, where she purchased oil that made her skin smell like rain.

Annabel R. took her new dress and her new scent and her new walk into a rough bar, where the boys wore barrels and spoke in verse, and she intoxicated these boys with a charm they had never seen.

The ugliest barrel boy spoke the prettiest verse and when he saw Annabel R. walk into the bar, he spoke and she heard him say that rain and revolution just walked through the door.

Annabel R. swooned, then regained her composure. She ordered red wine, took a pen off the counter, and wrote *Revolution* on the tag inside the dress where the washing instructions would normally be.

83. Wet Green Blades High as His Hips

Once again, security woke Zachary R. from his slumber on the aisle of concrete in the outdoor nursery. What seemed strange to him, though, was that he wasn't arrested either time, even though this time, there was a shopping cart full of building materials left in the exact middle of the store. Zachary R. was perplexed by the look of abject pity on the security guard's face as he escorted Zachary R. out of the store for the second time.

The security guard released Zachary R.'s arm once they were outside, and then his look took on another characteristic. It was now abject pity coupled with halfhearted hardness.

"Sir, I'm truly sorry you have nowhere else to sleep. I'm truly sorry you're homeless. My brother has a mental illness, so I know how difficult it is for you people. But I'm afraid if I catch you in here again, I'm going to have you arrested. Please, if you can, get some help."

Zachary R. was indignant. "Nowhere to sleep? Homeless? Mental illness? Who did that security guard think he was talking to?" he thought.

He pushed these questions deep inside, where they took up residence with his mother and father, his wife, and Bernrd Red—all of whom were gone, never to be seen again, but not gone away, not dealt with.

Zachary R. set off on foot, intending to go north into the New Hampshire mountains to atone for the deaths of his mother and his wife.

"I like rivers and women," he said and headed south by mistake.

He headed south by mistake along the river and south along a tributary of the river and south along smaller and smaller tributaries of the river until he heard the sound of a plane, which made him look at the sky, which was now dark.

He looked into the night sky and saw a thousand stars. He continued to look into the night sky. He saw ten thousand stars and the moon. He continued to look into the night sky. He saw knights, rooks, and bishops.

Zachary R. walked south along a tributary looking into the night sky when he felt something fluffy squirm beneath his feet and then, in conjunction with the squirming, he smelled a powerful yet satisfying, odor.

He looked down just in time to see the white stripe of a skunk vanish into the wet green blades along the tributary.

Zachary R. followed the white stripe into the wet green blades high as his hips the secondhand light of the moon upon the skunk's stripe which lured him to a ledge that descended to the sea and he followed the stripe over the ledge and into the crashing tide that tossed him around and thrashed him about and spat him back onto the shore.

Zachary R. woke the next morning covered with vicious greenhead flies. If it weren't for his heavy coat, his entire body would have been covered with welts and swelling and pain, but as luck would have it, he only suffered bites on his cheeks, neck, and the fleshy part between the bridge of his nose and his eyes.

He stood up and scraped his salty wet clothes with a stick. Then he climbed up the ledge, which was more like a sandbar only a few yards high, and he walked back through the wet green blades high as his hips, and when he returned to the tributary, he started south again but he couldn't remember why.

And then he began to chant, "Service to Mankind, Service to Mankind," which made him recall that his mission was to the north.

Zachary R. turned around and set off on foot toward the New Hampshire mountains where the traveler had pulled to the side of the road to help him so many years before.

84. Hobbes Scholar with a Nose Ring

Sarah R. wore the Revolution Dress as often as she could. Kids at school began to take notice, and not in a negative way. She seemed to possess some kind of mysterious power over them and over herself. The power was the newfound self-sufficiency thrust upon her by circumstance, along with the unique style and peculiar shade of burgundy of the dress and the secret word written on the tag inside: "Revolution."

She began to take risks. She pierced her nose and wore a nose ring. She put rings through her eyebrows and in rows along the tops of her ears.

She began driving the Nova, as her father had instructed. This increased her popularity immensely. She drove her friends everywhere, sometimes charging them for gas money and a little extra for her time. Rock concerts and record stores, boyfriends' and girlfriends' houses, rounding up friends and bringing them back to her house for parties, since her father was gone.

The neighbors began to take notice, but for a time they attributed her behavior to the ever-increasing absence of her father. They thought that once he got a new job and otherwise righted himself, things would return to normal.

Sarah R. also became charitable.

She donated blood to the Red Cross. She volunteered at a pet shelter and learned how to vaccinate the kittens. She volunteered at the rehab hospital in hopes that her father would appear there, but in the meantime, she intoxicated the junkies with the opiate of her charm and the Revolution Dress.

As the days passed, the police and child services department began to take notice. While Sarah R. did an adequate job maintaining the inside of the house, the front lawn did not receive the attention Zachary R. had given it with his mower. Their New England lawn began to grow long and thick and green with blades that grew high as her hips.

Social workers began to visit with greater and greater frequency to inquire about her well-being and about the whereabouts of her father, but Sarah R. was always able to demonstrate the adequacy of her circumstances by showcasing the food in the cupboard, the clean surroundings, and the maintenance of her grades at school.

In this regard, Sarah R. particularly excelled. Sarah R. was no little match girl. She was curious and rapidly lost any semblance of naiveté. She had no problem figuring out how to handle her homework dilemma while at the same time earning extra money to supplement the money she was receiving from her "chauffeur" service.

Sarah R. convinced the owner-proprietor of the local bookstore to hire her and pay her under the table, since she was still without a social security number.

The bookstore owner took an avuncular interest in Sarah and, understanding her circumstances, paid her far too much for the work she did, which was shelving books for a few hours a week.

Sarah R. was curious about many things, one of which was the disturbing thoughts of philosophers. With the help of the bookstore owner, she was able to understand and relate to much of what they had to say.

Sarah R.'s favorite philosopher was Thomas Hobbes.

Solitary, poor, nasty, brutish, and short. These were just about the least sentimental and the truest words she could imagine to describe life. With the help of the bookstore owner, she made the study of Hobbes her hobby. And the bookstore owner paid her well and helped her with her homework, even doing entire algebra assignments if she was really struggling.

Sarah R. wasn't above cheating. She wasn't above mooching. Honing such skills was essential to survival in her Hobbesian world.

85. Deep Depression, Bitter Fool

Zachary R. passed by his house en route to the New Hampshire mountains, too embarrassed to see his daughter in his condition of dirt and fly bites and ratty overcoat. He scoffed at the Cold Angel when she appeared. He lashed out at her for making a fool of him, for her being a figment and a fraud, for deceiving him, for making him quit his job and becoming an embarrassment to his daughter and to himself.

When he passed right by his house, the neighbors didn't recognize him.

Sarah R. saw him coming up the street from the living room window. She went into the kitchen to get cleaning supplies to quickly clean up before he walked through the door. She rearranged the furniture, threw the Revolution Dress into the laundry bin, vacuumed the carpets, washed the dirty dishes, and sponged the walls with mild dish soap.

Sarah R. became so engrossed in her cleaning that before she knew it, an hour had gone by and her father had not walked through the door.

She broke inside.

She grabbed a hammer and began pounding divots into the freshly sponged walls. She busted and pounded until the vicious energy was gone. Then she went into the attic and fell asleep in the dirty and wrinkled Revolution Dress.

Meanwhile, Zachary R. kept heading north toward the New Hampshire mountains. He wanted redemption. He wanted to revisit the picnic grounds where his mother had collapsed on the hard dirt and where the traveler had helped him. He wanted to keep alive his chances to become a Messiah or Rock Star.

But when he arrived, he found that the place held no honest significance. It was dead, indifferent. His life had gone off on this destructive tangent, and it was too late to get back what he had.

Zachary R. crouched under a picnic table and waited for the thud of a falling pine cone.

86. A Moment of Clarity

The Cold Angel sat beside Zachary R. under the picnic table and rubbed his back like winter. Zachary R. felt the shivers bloom inside of him. Acute rattling, acute comfort.

He looked at the Cold Angel and said, "Sometimes the shivers are painful, but you make the shivers feel good. And also, what am I doing here?"

"Service to mankind," she said.

"No," said Zachary R. "That makes no sense. I am here because of the boxcars and the endless train. My mother never recovered from her fall from when I told that story. Even after that traveler and I got her home, she was never the same. She just lay there in bed in that tissue-fiber nightgown and moaned and glared all day long and that fucking parrot and my father who cared only for chess and my pregnant wife and that sleazebag Bernrd Red cheating on my honeymoon.

"I'm here because I want to change the past. Service to mankind has nothing to do with it. Service to mankind is bullshit."

The Cold Angel ran her veil over his scalp and said, "You have been lying to yourself for a long time, but you don't have to suffer anymore. Goodbye, Zachary," she said and disappeared into the fog.

PART XII

87. Leaves of Absence

It looked like Easter clouds on the morning after the Cold Angel, though the New Hampshire trees told him it was autumn. Zachary R. paused and then proclaimed, "Leaves of Absence."

His bites still hurt and his overcoat was still ratty and malodorous, but he felt clean inside and his mind was clear.

He took a quick inventory of his circumstances: The mission was a fraud. He had no job. His adolescent daughter was home alone.

Zachary R. set off on foot toward home thinking, "I like rivers and women."

He arrived home on a thin autumn Monday, only slightly drunk and feeling good about making a new start.

The first thing he noticed as he approached the front door was the condition of the front lawn: green blades high as his hips.

"I'll mow it this Saturday after I get my old job back," he thought.

Zachary R. arrived at the front door of his house expecting to have to knock and wait for his daughter to greet him and let him inside.

To his slight dismay, however, the door was unlocked. He let himself in and announced his presence to ensure that he didn't startle Sarah.

There was no response to his voice. He went room to room searching for Sarah. She was nowhere to be found.

He went into the master bedroom and lay down on the bed. He heard sounds coming from the ceiling. Thuds and squeaks.

He got up and went into the closet with the entrance to the attic. He climbed up the ladder and pushed open the attic door.

Sarah R. screamed. "Dad, what the hell!?"

Zachary R. beheld his daughter. Sarah R. sat cross-legged on the attic floor, head shaved, wearing her mother's burgundy dress, the urn on her left, the cigar box on her right, a copy of

Hobbes' *Leviathan* in her hand, and the words *solitary, poor, nasty, brutish,* and *short* written in melted wax on the attic floor.

Zachary R.'s mind muddied and his insides churned. He felt chilled and nauseated.

Without uttering a sound, he climbed back down the closet ladder and ran for the bathroom. He grabbed the flyswatter and recited the words: forehand, backhand, microphone, guitar, spider on shoulder, cockroach on soap bar slipping, slipping, slipping. One violent dry heave. He grabbed his haunches and moved his knees to his chest.

Sarah R. knelt beside him, placed her hand on his shoulder, collapsed on him, and embraced him until he slept.

* * * * *

Zachary R. awoke in his own bed on Tuesday morning, a breakfast tray on the nightstand: toast, grapefruit, coffee, orange juice.

He was still shaken by the sight of his daughter in the attic, but if she still loved him enough to bring him breakfast in bed, how bad could she be? He cleaned himself up and dressed for his return to work.

Zachary R. drove the Nova downtown to the Law Offices of Miller & Associates, which was located in the fourth-largest skyscraper in Boston.

He rode the elevator to the top floor, where the file room was located, went into the boss's office, and asked for his old job back.

To his mild displeasure, the boss and his two fellow file clerks were happy to have him back, as they had been unable to find a replacement for him who lasted more than a week.

A small part of Zachary R. was relieved that the safety and routine of a day-to-day job had been returned to him, but a larger part of him died inside when he saw those files with their twelve-digit numbering scheme.

He managed to get through Tuesday and Wednesday without too much resistance, but by Thursday morning, thoughts of the Cold Angel and the mission began to stir.

He spent most of Thursday at the photocopier on the floor below daydreaming about his recent adventures, which now didn't seem so onerous. He had forgotten about betraying his daughter's trust and the bad burger in the shed and the vicious greenhead flies and being thrashed about in the freezing ocean tide.

All he could remember was the freedom and the reclamation of his identity as an aspiring Messiah or Rock Star.

By the time of his commute home on Thursday evening, the moment of clarity he had that past weekend had all but vanished. Zachary R. felt agitated and restless. It took every ounce of willpower not to stop inside the bar for seven drinks.

The sight of Sarah when he walked through the door gave him all of five minutes of relief, but her head was still bald and she had not taken off her mother's dress. Zachary R.'s agitation returned. And his nausea. He tried to sleep it off, but dry heaves kept coming all night long. He stuck the handle of the flyswatter down his throat to no avail. Dry heaves. Tap water helped a little, but the retching continued. Pain and fatigue. His entire body began to shake.

It was five o'clock on Friday morning when Zachary R. coughed blood into the toilet and it formed the shape of a rose.

He passed out. Minutes later he was awoken by seven pale girls who had circled him, raising their lockets to cover their giggling faces. One of them, a redhead with black lips, who was somewhat gorgeous, lay down beside him and wrapped her arms around him. Warmth and comfort replaced pain and nausea. He fell back to sleep, peacefully.

The next time Zachary R. woke, the girls vanished. He made his way to the living room and called in sick to his boss.

He spent the whole day on the living room sofa recovering, looking out the window at the tall green blades in the front lawn.

"I will mow tomorrow at halftime," he thought.

88. Committed Revisited

Zachary R. slept well through the night and woke late on Saturday morning.

His stomach felt better. His head was clear. He was very hungry. He went into the kitchen and opened the refrigerator, but it was warm and empty, except for a grapefruit and a Hershey's chocolate bar.

Zachary R. closed the refrigerator and saw a Post-It note from Sarah R. stuck to the door. The note read: "Went to the blood drive. Took the Nova. Unplugged the fridge to save on the electric bill. Feel free to plug it back in since you are back now and we are both working. See you this afternoon. Sarah."

Zachary R. reached behind the refrigerator and plugged it in. His stomach growled and his mind went blank for lack of food.

He went into the living room and turned on the television. College football. Nebraska at Boston College. Early in the first quarter. He stared at the television for a moment, and then made a decision to walk down to the Burger Shack to get a burger to go so he could return and watch the game.

Zachary R. made it to the Burger Shack and back without incident, except for brief flashes and afterimages of the brown bag with the bad burger that he had partially eaten and tossed in disgust onto the hard dirt floor of the abandoned shed on the riverbank. He felt pity for this lonely burger that he had left to rot alone in the shed. The searing mental sun beat down hard through the thin autumn air.

As he sat in the living room of his house, eating the good Burger Shack burger and watching the football game, he began to feel guilty. The desire to care for the bad burger, to restore it to edibility, became unbearably urgent.

Luckily, however, the game reached halftime and he recalled that it was time to mow the front lawn, green blades high as his hips. He forgot about the bad burger once the mowing began.

In fact, his concentration on leveling the lawn was so singular, so intense, that it never wavered, even as the Nova swerved down the street, ran over the curb, and barreled through the front yard. He didn't look up from the mower until he heard the Nova crash through the living room window.

Zachary R. cut the engine and ran inside. Sarah R. had already exited the car and was brushing glass and other debris off herself when Zachary R. entered what was left of the living room.

Love and calm and clarity overwhelmed him.

"What happened, Sarah?" he asked. "Are you all right?"

"I am so sorry, Dad," she cried, visibly shaken and pale. "I was driving home from donating at the Red Cross and all of the blood in my head went to my feet. I must have passed out."

Zachary R. recalled his advice to her about the virtues of donating blood to fight evil men. He felt proud of her and ashamed of himself at the same time. The black sun of empathy shined inside of him and seemed to illuminate the debris in the house.

"It's okay, Sarah," he said softly. "It's okay."

He kissed her and sent her to her room with the grapefruit and the Hershey's from the fridge. Then he set about surrounding the house with orange cones to distract the eyes of the neighbors.

Pitiful thoughts of the bad burger— half-eaten, lonely, and festering in the abandoned shed—returned with merciless ferocity. He wanted to care for it, so he set off on foot saying, "Service to mankind, Service to mankind."

The Goth Girls watched in amazement as Zachary R., with superhuman tenacity and endurance, walked for eight miles, ducking into tenements, ripping numbers off of doors and feeding them, nails and all, into his desperate and bleeding mouth. The tenants screamed and tilted and spoke in tongues as they beheld Zachary R. in his psychotic ecstasy. The Goth Girls clutched their Damien lockets and swooned at the gory sight of it all.

Zachary R. wound up in the hardware store for the third time. The security guard had no choice but to keep his word and hold him for arrest or at least get him to a hospital to care for his bleeding mouth.

A month later, in the asylum, Zachary R. claimed to the Cracked Snail, "I have Neosporin . . . ."

89. Mind of Science Versus Mind of Zachary

The doctors and nurses in the asylum did their best to eradicate the worms, microbes, and malodor in Zachary R.'s mind. "It's like pulling out the innards of a pumpkin," said Zachary R. when the nurses asked him how his treatment was going.

These men and women, this collective mind of science, worked diligently to rehabilitate Zachary R. Psychotherapy, antipsychotics, pain killers, and antidepressants were generously prescribed, dispensed, and administered. Droperidol. Haloperidol. Lorazepam. Diazepam. Paxil. Prozac. And more.

Several forms of occupational therapy were also attempted.

Crossword puzzles met with marginal success.

Jigsaw puzzles saw a slight regression.

Chess necessitated a lockdown of the entire premises as Zachary R. flung the board and the pieces across the room, hitting a paranoid schizophrenic and inciting an all-patient melee. Heavy doses of sedatives and antipsychotics were administered to all.

Finally, it occurred to the mind of science to ask Zachary R. what he liked, to which he responded, "I like rivers and women."

While the doctors were satisfied and the nurses bewitched by this answer, it was not the answer they were looking for. They rephrased the question to, "What kinds of activities do you enjoy?" Zachary R.'s immediate reply was "mowing the lawn."

The mind of science was pleased with this answer. Within two weeks, authority had been given, forms had been signed, and Zachary R. was out on the asylum lawn assisting the gardening staff with mowing duties—which were called privileges—for the rest of his days inside.

90. The Cracked Snail's Portrait

Zachary R. sat in the exact middle of the asylum lawn on a chair that made a pattern on his legs. He knew that if he stared long enough into the grass, he would see a glint in the blades under the searing mental sun and then the Cracked Snail would come into focus.

And each time, without fail, the Cracked Snail would say, "With that level of concentration, you could paint my portrait, which I would like very much." So, one day, Zachary R. brought a box of colored pencils with him onto the asylum lawn and tried to draw the Cracked Snail's portrait.

Using exclusively the yellow pencil, Zachary R. drew the spiral of the snail's shell, including a jagged line to indicate where the crack was.

Each time he showed the drawing to the Cracked Snail, it replied: "Your style is in the manner of the universal minimalists or the minimal universalists. Simplicity and grandiosity,

Messiah and Rock Star, both are conveyed in your work."

Each time Zachary R. heard the Cracked Snail's assessment, he would smile, fold the drawing into eighths, put it into his pocket, and then later shut it inside a drawer in his room.

After thirty-four spirals with jagged lines were drawn, something more began to appear in the portraits. Around the spiral, still with the yellow pencil, Zachary R. drew a tilted triangle. Inside the tilted triangle was a set of double doors, like cellar doors, and reaching to open the double doors, a tall, thin figure with a right-angle chin and eyes that blossomed like sunflowers.

Soon the thirty-four spirals became fifty-five spirals with tilted triangles, which became eighty-nine tilted triangles with double doors, which became one hundred and forty-four tall, thin figures reaching to open the double doors, all in searing yellow pencil folded into eighths and placed inside a drawer in his room.

91. Kittens and Heroin

Stardust in her backpack. Flask in her pocket. Opium in her veins.

In the months after her father was committed to the asylum, Sarah R., in order, stopped going to school, adopted a kitten, and took up heroin.

But she didn't quit her job at the bookstore. Although the bookstore owner was a positive influence on Sarah R. in most respects, he did have his shortcomings, one of which was a burgeoning heroin habit. To his credit, however, he kept his stash hidden from Sarah and didn't catch on that she was the reason his supplies were dwindling more rapidly than normal until he noticed her nodding off in the middle of their discussions on Hobbes.

Having seen this telltale sign, he instantly knew to examine her arms, which were defaced by fledgling needle tracks.

"Trust me, Sarah," he said, "you don't want to develop a junk habit. It'll kill you. It's killing me."

"But it feels so good, like a feather boa or ashes dusting my face, or like I'm Jesus' daughter," she replied.

The bookstore owner smirked. "How Lou Reed of you," he said.

"Sarah," he said with avuncular concern, "I'm afraid you won't be able to work here anymore. I don't want you developing a habit. I couldn't live with myself."

The bookstore owner reached into his desk drawer to retrieve his checkbook. He handed Sarah R. a substantial check as severance.

Sarah R. pocketed the check, hugged the bookstore owner, swiped his stash, ran home, pet the kitten, finished off the bourbon in her flask, shaved her head, climbed the ladder into the attic, jumped into the Revolution Dress, and overdosed.

92. Trick-or-Treating with Foster Parents

The overdose would have ended Sarah R.'s time on Earth had the child services department been less diligent in placing a social worker to drop by regularly until proper foster parents could be found.

Not only did the social worker know CPR, but she also owned a car. The social worker greeted Sarah when she arrived home from the bookstore, saw her climb the ladder into the attic, and felt the music thumping above her.

As the social worker prepared their dinner, she noticed that the CD had begun to skip with machine-like speed and metronomic precision. She waited for the thumping to resume, but five minutes passed and there was no change in sound or feel.

The social worker climbed the ladder into the attic and saw Sarah's motionless body lying limp and heavy on the attic floor next to a spoon, a burner, and a syringe.

She choked with helplessness. She could perform CPR and make all efforts to keep Sarah breathing, but there was no way she could get her down the ladder and into her car to take her to the hospital emergency room.

The social worker revived Sarah R. and turned her on her side, slid down the ladder, sprained both ankles on landing, crawled to the phone, and dialed 911.

The paramedics arrived in seven minutes, revived Sarah R. again, and took her to the emergency room for overnight observation.

The ER doctors believed the overdose was intentional. They intended to admit Sarah to the asylum for observation and counseling, but Sarah, not wanting to be anywhere near her father, convinced them it was a horrible accident, that she was just experimenting with the macabre because of Halloween, which was a week away, and accidentally overdosed.

The doctors didn't find this story believable in the least, but they sent her home anyway because they agreed among themselves that it would not be in her best interest to be anywhere near her father.

Sarah R. stayed overnight in the hospital and was driven home the next afternoon by her new foster parents.

* * * * *

In later years, Sarah R. didn't recall much about her foster parents except that they were kind to her and to her kitten. "Kind people never leave much of an impression," she lamented. She also recalled that they let her be a junkie that Halloween even though she had just overdosed the week before.

"They laughed at the horrified expressions on the faces of the neighbors when they laid eyes on my junkie makeup and my needle tracks, which were real," she said.

93. The Notorious Dr. Beverly Farworthy

Mostly the mind of science sought Zachary R.'s rehabilitation, but sometimes minds have tumors. One such tumor on the mind of science was the notorious Dr. Beverly Farworthy.

When Zachary R. learned that he had been scheduled for a session with Dr. Farworthy, he asked the other patients in the dayroom about her. The patients complained about Dr. Farworthy's unorthodox methods; about how she would examine patient histories to find their most hideous demons and then, rather than assuage them, she would exploit them. Dr. Farworthy believed this approach worked because, much like an exorcism, the patient's demons were forcibly and immediately brought out into the light where they could be subdued and defeated.

Dr. Farworthy's approach was controversial, yet from time to time it yielded tremendous results. Had she not had the unattractive habit of ingesting high-dose ecstasy before her sessions, she could have become a celebrity doctor.

"Zachary," said Dr. Farworthy, before he even had a chance to sit down, "can you tell me why you didn't respect yourself enough to deal with your cheating wife?" Without time to think of a proper answer, Zachary R. replied, "I was isolating and surviving. I was trying to win."

"Could you repeat that?" asked Dr. Farworthy.

"I was isolating and surviving, I was . . ."

"Trying to win," she said, finishing the thought for him. "Now, tell me about the incident on your honeymoon." Zachary R. spared no details in his description of the events on the day of his betrayal, including the name he saw on the concierge badge, "Bernrd Red." On hearing this name, Dr. Farworthy's eyes lit up. And then the ecstasy took over and the doctor, without giving it a second thought, began to divulge confidential patient information.

"Did you know Bernrd Red was a patient of mine?" she asked. "He came through here thirteen years ago and I was responsible for curing him. What happened on your honeymoon was the tip of the iceberg with Bernrd Red. He was ultraviolent. Not just with his lovers, and not to diminish the pain he caused you, of course," said Dr. Farworthy, rambling on.

Zachary R. turned gray. Still standing, he clutched the back of the analysand chair with such force that the cheap upholstery began to tear.

When Dr. Farworthy proudly showed him the scar Bernrd Red had given her during one of their sessions, Zachary R. went berserk, smashing up her office and attacking her.

A month later, after the investigation had been completed, Dr. Farworthy was summarily dismissed and her license to practice psychiatry revoked. Her last act as a psychiatrist was an act of retaliation. Dr. Farworthy told Zachary R. that he was a violent sleazebag just like Bernrd

Red, and that Zachary R. was sleeping in the same bed in the asylum that Bernrd Red slept in. She was lying, of course, but Zachary R., of course, believed her.

94. Bernrd Red's Former Bed

Zachary R. sat up in what he believed was Bernrd Red's former bed, unbearably awake because of his honeymoon.

He alternated between talking to himself, remembering chess with his father, and having imaginary quarrels and fistfights with Bernrd Red. All of these were catalyzed by varying dosages of antipsychotics and sedatives and painkillers, which had the following side effects:

Queens and pawns.

Wind chimes and lavender.

Knights and bishops.

Savage splendor.

He imagined that Sarah handed him the urn. He opened it and stared at the ashes, searching for humanity.

95. The Cracked Snail's Opinion

Zachary R. was beside himself after his visit with the notorious Dr. Beverly Farworthy, convinced she was telling the truth that he was sleeping in the same bed that Bernrd Red slept in.

He wanted confirmation from a known trustworthy source.

Zachary R. sat in the exact middle of the asylum lawn on a chair that made a pattern on his legs, staring urgently into the green blades and hoping to see the Cracked Snail.

He fidgeted and scratched at his arms. He hummed Haydn. His mind buzzed under the searing mental sun like bees in a lavender bush, until at last he fell asleep. He woke an hour later, still seated in his chair, with a neckache and a sunburn, when the Cracked Snail finally appeared.

"I apologize for the delay," said the Cracked Snail. "I'm afraid my wound has been extra painful today and I have overindulged on poison pellets. I must have passed out in the asylum garden."

"Apology accepted," said Zachary R.

"You look anxious," said the Cracked Snail. "What's on your mind?"

"Was there ever a patient here named Bernrd Red?" asked Zachary R.

"Yes," said the Cracked Snail. "He came through here about thirteen years ago. He wore a ruby ring. He made the nurses sweat."

"What was your opinion of him?" asked Zachary R. "Are he and I similar? Dr. Farworthy told me I remind her of him."

"Dr. Farworthy is a liar," said the Cracked Snail. "The only similarity between the two of you is your high intensity. But your high intensity is inspiring and sincere, and his was just stupid and violent. I never cared for Bernrd Red."

Zachary R.'s eyes blossomed like sunflowers. "Thank you," he said.

"Anytime," said the Cracked Snail.

96. The Cracked Snail's Soliloquy

The Cracked Snail slithered among the blades of the asylum lawn, singing this song to the patients:
"There are many worlds in which to live,
choose the one with the most to give.
"There are many minds in which to fight,
ignore your mind and do what's right."

97. Forgiveness

Zachary R. lay in bed in the asylum feeling unwanted pity for Bernrd Red, who had suffered in this same asylum thirteen years earlier. But no matter what he did, no matter what contradictory and violent thoughts he had for Bernrd, the black sun of empathy refused to dim.

Zachary R. tossed and turned and shivered through the night until, finally, his mind gave out. He heard footsteps coming down the hall and stopping at his door, the door opening. Bernrd Red shined a flashlight at Zachary R. "Can you forgive me?" he asked.

Zachary R. sat up in bed and muttered, "Yes." His eyes blossomed like sunflowers.

"Just kidding," said Bernrd Red. "I'm not asking for your forgiveness. You'll never learn, will you?"

Zachary R. felt the sensation of being hit in the head with a rock. He bull-rushed Bernrd Red and drove him out the door and into the hall.

Then he shoved Bernrd Red down the hall and out onto the asylum lawn, where seven women were waiting in lab coats to escort him off the premises.

PART XIII

98. A Letter

Zachary R. sat in his room examining each of the one hundred and forty-four portraits of the Cracked Snail when an orderly kindly interrupted to inform him that a letter awaited him in the asylum mailroom.

The orderly escorted him through the dayroom, across the asylum lawn in the searing mental sun, and finally past intake and into the mailroom, where the mail attendant handed him an open envelope with a letter from Sarah R. inside.

The orderly unfolded a chair and motioned for Zachary R. to sit and read the letter, which was written in all caps and read like a telegram:

DAD:

HOPE YOU ARE WELL. I'M OKAY. WORN OUT MY WELCOME WITH THE FOSTER PARENTS. DON'T BE ANGRY AT THEM. THEY'RE NICE PEOPLE. SAINTS. I AM TAKING THE URN, MOM'S DRESS, AND

THE NOVA TO LA. I WOULD COME SEE YOU, BUT IT'S STILL TOO HARD. GET WELL. DON'T BE TOO HARD ON YOURSELF.

LOVE, SARAH

P.S. BAD NEWS ABOUT THE HOUSE. FORECLOSURE.

"Can I keep this?" asked Zachary R.

The mailroom attendant looked at her supervisor. The supervisor nodded.

Zachary R. put the letter back inside the envelope, folded the entire apparatus in half, and put it in his pocket.

Back in his room, Zachary R. emptied the drawer with the one hundred and forty-four portraits of the Cracked Snail and put the letter inside. He slipped the portraits under the mattress.

99. Dr. Russell Keating

Zachary R.'s behavior began to improve after he read the letter from Sarah, for both heroic and practical reasons. Not only did he want to go on a quest to L.A. in search of his daughter, but also he wanted to try to save his home.

The dismissal of Dr. Farworthy also helped. Her replacement, Dr. Russell Keating, was far more qualified to care for Zachary R., if for no better reason than he sincerely desired Zachary R.'s recovery.

Dr. Keating was the rose to Dr. Farworthy's thorn, the healthy tissue to her tumor on the mind of science. Dr. Keating, for example, understood the healing properties of Zachary R.'s mowing the asylum lawn. A routine had been established whereby Zachary R. would say, "I like rivers and women" and Dr. Keating would grant him permission to mow the asylum lawn. This state of events was agreeable for doctor and patient, as well as for asylum management, which saved on gardening expenses.

Zachary R. had now been in the asylum fifteen months and all indications were that his release was imminent. He took his meds. He attended his sessions with Dr. Keating. He spoke with the Cracked Snail and drew its portrait. He mowed the asylum lawn. And each night before bed, he read the letter from Sarah.

Dr. Keating reported Zachary R.'s progress to the board, specifically noting his affinity for rivers and women. The board agreed with the doctor that Zachary R. was ready to return to society.

100. The Next to Last Night at the House

It looked like Easter clouds on the day of Zachary R.'s release from the asylum. Dr. Keating shook Zachary R.'s hand and pulled him to his bony body for a rickety hug.

Zachary R. packed his clothes, the portraits of the Cracked Snail, and the letter from Sarah. An orderly appeared at the door with a wheelchair and wheeled the whole apparatus, including Zachary R., out of the asylum and back into the world.

The clouds cleared and, though it was winter, the sky seemed hot under the searing mental sun. Zachary R. felt good. His mind was quiet and his resolve was strong. His plan to sell the house and head west to find his daughter was both logical and the right thing to do.

The asylum shuttle service dropped Zachary R. off in the driveway of his house. He was relieved to see that measures had been taken to board up the living room window and that the lawn had been watered and mowed in his absence.

When Zachary R. walked through the front door, which had been left unlocked, he found five envelopes lying in the entryway. The first envelope contained the key to the house. The second envelope contained a note from the neighbors confirming that they had been doing basic upkeep and that the gardener—Annabel R.'s erstwhile paramour—had been maintaining the front lawn. The third envelope was from the U.S. Postal Service, informing him that his mail was being held at the post office. The fourth envelope was from Sarah R., confirming what she had written in her letter, that she had gone to "LA" and that the house was in foreclosure. The fifth envelope was a subscription offer from *Playboy* magazine.

Suddenly Zachary R.'s mind became noisy with worry over home and daughter. He set off on foot to the post office to retrieve his mail, which consisted almost entirely of past-due notices on the house.

He considered the definition of insanity: "to do the same thing over and over and expect different results." He went to the bar anyway.

The bartender immediately recognized Zachary R. and recalled his pattern of behavior, which was to confront the customers with his cryptic statements, such as:

"Cigar boxes and romance novels are the brass knuckles of sex."

Or, "I am nostalgic for the dark-road signature of the skunk."

Or, "Are you lonely as the cello? No, I am lonely as an aisle of concrete in the moonlight."

The bartender firmly pulled Zachary R. aside and explained that Zachary could stay in the bar and drink so long as he kept his mouth shut. Zachary R. promptly agreed to these terms. In the spirit of compromise, the bartender poured Zachary R. three double shots of Wild Turkey and sent him out the back door.

Zachary R. returned home, grabbed his suitcase, and climbed into the attic. He dumped the contents of the suitcase onto the attic floor, scattered the portraits of the Cracked Snail, and passed out.

101. The Last Night at the House Revisited

Zachary R. came to the next afternoon in the sweltering attic, sweating bourbon and shaking violently. His head throbbed and his mouth was dry.

He climbed down from the attic, knowing he would be leaving for good that night. He took a quick inventory of what he would be able to take with him to L.A.

There was no food in the cupboards and the fridge was warm and empty.

No furniture could come, of course.

There were no toiletries in the bathrooms, though the flyswatter still hung from a hook on the wall by the toilet.

Zachary R. carefully removed the flyswatter from its hook and carried it up the ladder into the attic, where he packed his clothes, the letter from Sarah, and the flyswatter. Finally, he gathered the one hundred and forty-four portraits of the Cracked Snail and packed one hundred and forty-three of them in his suitcase. He unfolded the last portrait and placed it in the exact middle of the attic. He took his suitcase and climbed down from the attic for the last time.

Zachary R. dropped the suitcase in the boarded-up living room and slept on the sofa until the sun went down.

When he woke, he took one final pass through the house. Everything seemed to be in order, except for the toilet, which he had forgotten to flush in his drunken stupor. He flushed the toilet and sterilized the seat with a sponge and rubbing alcohol.

Toilet was sterilized. Flyswatter was packed. Fridge was warm and empty. Asylum was in the past.

Zachary R. closed the door of his house for the last time . . . .

102. All the Unlocked Doors

How was it possible,
all the unlocked doors?

Was it the Goth Girls
or unknown others?

Was it a failure of body,
every nerve scraped and startled,
or confusion of mind,

every memory ambiguous and addled?

How was it possible,
all the unlocked doors?

103. A Boxcar Journey to L.A., Part 1

Zachary R. woke the following morning next to a stack of pine logs outside his former house, which now had busted windows in addition to the boarded-up living room window, and new divots pounded into the walls in addition to the divots his daughter had pounded.

He grabbed his suitcase and set off on foot to the hardware store.

Zachary R. was hopeful that the security guard there would take pity on his circumstances and give him bus fare for the trip to L.A.

Zachary R. had no money. He had signed forms in the asylum that gave the relevant authorities the power to pay his bills during his stay. By the time of his release, Zachary R.'s meager savings had been depleted. No money. No house. No car.

The moment Zachary R. walked through the door of the hardware store, he was turned around and escorted out by the familiar security guard, who was clearly a man of his word. Zachary R. didn't even have an opportunity to grunt. Nor did he protest with his fists. Instead, he set off on foot to the Boston rail yard, where he boarded a boxcar and headed west.

104. A Nova Journey to New Orleans

As indicated in her letter, Sarah R. packed the urn and the Revolution Dress and took the Nova to LA. But by "LA," she didn't mean Los Angeles, but rather Louisiana—and specifically, New Orleans.

Sarah knew her father would misinterpret the letter to mean Los Angeles, which meant he would not be able to find her. She also knew she would confuse her foster parents and the child services department. She was determined to start a new life without the false hope of her father recovering.

The Nova held up remarkably well, considering what she had put it through. The engine ran smoothly despite the busted-up grill and the missing headlight, which got her fix-it tickets in New Jersey, West Virginia, and Tennessee.

Each night she slept in the backseat, or rather, she lay awake in the backseat with mixed emotions. On the one hand, she felt shame and confusion. She opened the urn, searching for humanity in her mother's ashes and finding none. She thought about her father and felt ashamed for deceiving him about where she was headed, as well as for the fact that she couldn't muster the strength to be there for him on his release from the asylum. She worried that he would quickly become ill again without his daughter and with his house in foreclosure. On the other hand, she was free—free of the weight of her father's illness, free of the false pity of the neighbors, free of her do-gooder foster parents, free from school.

But she was also free of her kitten, which she gave to the bookstore owner. "Every bookstore needs a cat," he said, reassuring her that he would take care of it. He even named the cat Hobbes, which made her cry.

Sarah R. arrived in New Orleans in early February, on the Wednesday before Mardi Gras.

105. A Boxcar Journey to L.A., Part 2

At last, Zachary R. was onboard an endless train that passed through tunnels in hills with shacks and cigarettes and by pigeons perched majestically on telephone wires, some with human heads, which made him shiver and giggle.

He was onboard the endless train that sent his mother over the edge and onto the hard dirt of the New Hampshire forest and into a tissue-fiber nightgown.

Zachary R. smiled the eyeless smile of eradicated dreams. This was what he wanted all along. And why not?

All aboard!

He introduced the Goth Girls to the Cold Angel. He showed off his portraits of the Cracked Snail. He laughed forgivingly, condescendingly, about his wife and Bernrd Red. He checkmated his father.

After what seemed like a complete and different and better lifetime, the train arrived at the massive rail yard near downtown Los Angeles.

He disembarked and set off on foot toward the soft prison of Hollywood and the grim task of searching for his daughter, whom he had happily forgotten about on the train.

106. A Bus Ride to the Ocean

From Argos

a thousand years

to Bethlehem

from Bethlehem

two thousand years

to Boston

from Boston

a boxcar journey

to Hollywood

from Hollywood

a bus ride

to the ocean

in the searing mental sun

a procession of ghosts

and he joined it

like a raindrop joins

a river.

PART XIV

107. Sea Change

Dr. Farworthy would not have been kept on the asylum staff as long as she was, had it not been for her tremendous success in reforming Bernrd Red, who was diagnosed with paranoia and acute sociopathic tendencies.

A landmark case study was published in the *New England Journal of Medicine,* which demonstrated the efficacy of aggressive combination therapy involving twice-daily private talk therapy coupled with stimulants, which, the study showed, had the paradoxical effect of reducing symptoms and ultimately curing the patient.

The doctor was only too willing to show her colleagues her scar, admonishing them to be vigilant in the early going because stimulation could intensify symptoms.

The case study, of course, was completely bogus. Doctor after doctor got attacked by overstimulated, hyperanalyzed, paranoid, sociopathic patients.

But there was no denying Bernrd Red's transformation.

During his violent sessions with Dr. Farworthy, and for that matter, during his entire stay in the asylum, he heard nothing but Crosby, Stills, Nash & Young's "Carry On" running through his mind over and over and over, which was the reason why he had checked himself in in the first place, and which was the reason why he ultimately put a stop to the carnage. During his final session with Dr. Farworthy, and without explanation, Bernrd Red—rather than continue promoting the sensation of being hit in the head with a rock—kissed the doctor's cheek, stroked her hair, went to his room, and never beat anyone again.

After being discharged from the asylum, Bernrd Red moved to New Orleans, where he lived passive and uneasy, cantankerous and celibate. But the music was good in New Orleans, which made life tolerable.

Bernrd Red loved music.

108. Café Macabre and the Fortune Teller

Solitary, poor, nasty, brutish, and short.

Sarah R. repeated her Hobbesian mantra for inspiration as she searched for a job in New Orleans, bald head notwithstanding.

Even with Mardi Gras long over, there were abundant positions available in the clubs and bars, most of which would have hired Sarah even though she had only turned sixteen in December. But Sarah instinctively knew she wanted nothing to do with serving rowdy drunks.

She gave Café Du Monde a try. The first week went well enough, serving chicory coffee and beignets to tourists. But when Monday morning arrived after a weekend of drinking in the Dungeon and pondering the empty urn, Sarah R. just couldn't bring herself to go back.

Instead, she spent the day recuperating and then, on Tuesday, three weeks post Mardi Gras, she got a job at Café Macabre, which sold poetry chapbooks and voodoo dolls in addition to coffee and pastries. A fortune teller was stationed upstairs.

All new hires received a complimentary visit with the fortune teller, and Sarah visited with him on the night after her first shift ended.

Her first question for the fortune teller was, "Aren't you supposed to be a woman?"

The fortune teller replied, "Aren't young women supposed to have hair?"

Sarah R. frowned and then allowed a crack of a smile to creep through. "Never mind my past," she said. "What do you see in my future?"

With the utmost confidence and clarity of voice, the fortune teller replied, "You tricked your father. Your father is injured. Your father is dying."

109. A Cigarette Break

The string of bells jingled against the glass business door of Café Macabre when Sarah R. stepped outside for her cigarette break.

Freaked out by what the fortune teller said the night before, she leaned against a pole with chipped paint and faded stickers, and resolved to leave for L.A. first thing tomorrow morning.

She brought flame to paper and smoked her tobacco, flicking ashes into the eyes of the daisies that stayed open anyway and moved like her hair would have—if she weren't bald—in the direction of the wind that swept copper leaves along the dry black street.

Then up came Bernrd Red in flannel pajamas that snagged his sores and made him grimace.

He saw Sarah R. against her pole and said, "Wouldn't it be nice if you had some hair that could blow in the direction of the wind? . . . But carry on, I mean, at least you're not like me. I drink in the morning and sleep until sundown, and then I wake nervous as a bull thinking slow as cheese and I pace in my pajamas in silence except for the pebble in my slipper, which irritates the hell out of me and makes me moan, but at least I'm done beating my lovers and at least I'm done promoting the sensation of being hit in the head with a rock. Hosanna."

He reached into his pocket, grabbed a handful of pennies, and tossed them—along with his pinky ring—into the dry black street.

The string of bells jingled against the glass business door of Café Macabre when Sarah R. stepped back inside.

She said "Benediction" as she dropped the pennies and the ring one by one into her tip jar.

110. News from the Working Parts, Part 2

Zachary R. couldn't be sure how long he had lived in his alley between medium buildings. He couldn't recall what his daughter looked like. He couldn't recall the human details of his life, only the symbols and the figments of his imagination. Or, perhaps, the figments, at some point, became more real to him than the human details. He had crossed over to the other side, as it were.

After all he had been through since his arrival in Hollywood, it was no surprise that his search for Sarah had waned to the point of flat black sky. No moon, no stars. Just the occasional knight, rook, or bishop.

After his release from police custody and the hospital, all he could think about was the pain in his injured hand, which had traveled up his arm, into his shoulders, and finally his brain.

And, to add insult to his injured hand, he also suffered from adult-onset asthma from breathing bus fumes, rotting food, urine, and feces.

He sampled his fingers: semen on the index, beer on the middle, stardom on the ring, asthma on the pinky, murder on the thumb.

He searched along the boulevard, but he couldn't remember why. Pain was all that remained.

His chances for Messiah or Rock Star were gone.

111. The Goth Girls Hold Vigil

Zachary R. lay unconscious in his alley between medium buildings, dreaming about pine trees and leisure, the infection becoming ever more dire.

Seven Goth Girls dressed in lab coats encircled him, each holding a lit candle. The redhead approached him and dripped hot wax onto his forehead, waking him.

"You're somewhat gorgeous," she said. "Chess is nearly impossible."

The dirty, bloodied, wax-stained ice rink of Zachary R.'s face melted. "I love it when you quote the Cracked Snail," he said.

She continued, "I need to look far away to erase your naked image from my mind."

Zachary R. giggled terribly, then slipped back into unconsciousness.

The redhead heard the sound of a plane. She looked at the sky.

112. An Ambulance Journey to the Hospital

The next time Zachary R. regained consciousness was to the sound of the siren of the ambulance that transported him to the hospital. His pain was so severe now that it no longer bothered him.

On the contrary, his pain now induced alternating states of euphoria and lucidity, both of which gave him a sense of well-being.

The nurse in the emergency room hooked Zachary R. up to an IV with antibiotics and shot him full of morphine. He was admitted to the ICU the next morning.

In his lucid moments Zachary R. rang for the nurse to come and listen to him rhapsodize about his daughter. The nurse was kind and tried to reassure him that L.A. was a big city and that Sarah would be there any day now to see him. Zachary R. was kind, too, and agreed with the nurse, even though he knew he would never see his daughter again.

At the end of his second day in the ICU, Zachary R. inquired as to whether the hospital had a courtyard with grass. The nurse confirmed that this was so.

113. A Nova Journey to L.A., Part 1

First thing tomorrow morning arrived and the Nova was packed and ready for the trip west. This wasn't due to the urgency Sarah R. felt to find her father, though she felt plenty. Rather, it was because she had been living in the car since she nearly burned down the bargain motel.

She shaved her head in the rearview mirror, said a prayer for her father, and kissed the ground for her mother, whose body and Revolution Dress were forever ashes in New Orleans.

Then she paid a visit to the Dungeon to say goodbye to the Dungeon Master who doubled as a hot dog vendor, but, sadly, the Dungeon had closed for the morning and there wasn't time to search the streets for the man's hot dog cart. Sarah R. reached into her pocket and breathed a sigh of relief when she felt the familiar edges of his business card scrape against her fingers. She removed the card from her pocket and slipped it in her cleavage, a souvenir, a keepsake, an heirloom to be placed in a future family album.

* * * * *

Sarah R. cashed her final paycheck from Café Macabre, put gas in the Nova, set the empty urn at her side, and headed west on the I-10 in search of her father.

Texas was long and flat with trees scattered in the distance. Sarah R. fell in love with it. She was falling in love in general. She decided to let her hair grow, somehow knowing that her life was blooming as part of some master plan, some benevolent grand scheme.

On night one of her journey, she slept in San Antonio. On night two of her journey, she slept in El Paso. On day three, the day she intended to drive straight through to L.A., she stopped for lunch in Las Cruces, New Mexico, the city in which she would live the rest of her life.

114. Las Cruces

Sarah R. drove into Las Cruces, New Mexico, looking for a café like Café Macabre. The town mainly had Tex-Mex restaurants, but it was also a college town, so there was no shortage of coffee houses.

Interspersed among the Starbucks were some definite possibilities. There was Café Trieste, Café Voltaire, Café Sport, and then she saw Café Hobbes. Sarah R. parked the Nova and navigated her way through a gauntlet of students to get to Café Hobbes. The string of bells jingled against the glass business door when she stepped inside.

Sarah R. walked directly to the cashier, a good-looking youth about eighteen years old, whom she assumed was a college student.

Painted in searing yellow letters on the wall behind the cashier were the words *Solitary, Poor, Nasty, Brutish,* and *Short*. Sarah R. swooned and collapsed onto the counter, where she would have struck her bald head were it not for the lightning-quick and chivalrous hands of the cashier, who caught her head just before impact.

When she came to, she was lying on her back in a long wooden booth with the cashier seated next to her holding a tissue soaked in rubbing alcohol that he had waved under her nose to revive her.

"Are you okay?" asked the cashier. "I often have that effect on girls who see me for the first time. I should have tried to warn you somehow."

Sarah R. rolled her eyes. "I swooned because of Thomas Hobbes, not because of you. He's my favorite philosopher."

"He's a drag," said the cashier.

"You would say that," snorted Sarah R. "You're probably a frat boy with perfect grades, shiny happy parents, and a golden retriever back home. You're a story about a boy and his dog. Solitary, poor, nasty, brutish, and short. That's my mantra."

"You're a runaway, aren't you?" he asked.

"Well, kind of," she said. "More like I was run away from. My mom is dead. I scattered her ashes in New Orleans. And my dad is certified. No lie. He's in L.A. and he's very sick. That's where I'm headed, to L.A."

"I'm sorry to hear that," he said. His tone softened.

"I was a runaway not too long ago. I was planning on running away to Hollywood to become a movie star, but then my mom got this suicide note in the mail written by a runaway in Hollywood."

"That makes no sense at all," said Sarah R. "I'm leaving. Thanks for sparing me a concussion."

"Wait. Let me explain," he said. "My mom processes magazine subscriptions in Boulder, Colorado. That's where I'm from. The runaway mailed his suicide note in a business reply envelope for *Playboy* magazine. My mom made a photocopy of the note and gave it to me to convince me not to run away. It worked. The kid comes across as a narcissistic jerk, which is what I was. I carry the note in my pocket wherever I go. Here, let me read it to you."

The cashier reached into his back pocket and pulled out the suicide note of H. James Branhoover, which read as follows:

"And so I ran away to Hollywood. Bigger moths need bigger flames. I know after I jump off this building, the world will mourn and pandemonium and chaos will reign. For the record, my dad was a good-for-nothing banker and my mom was an abusive whore. Good riddance to them. Didn't they know who I was? Come to think of it, didn't any of you people know who I was? Fuck all of you! No longer yours, H. James Branhoover."

Sarah R. fell silent for a minute and then said, "I've never heard a real suicide note before. It's so sad." Then she allowed herself a small smile. "Bigger moths need bigger flames? What does that mean?"

The cashier laughed. "It's bullshit. Or maybe he thought he was Icarus," he said.

"That's beautiful," said Sarah R. "He was so delusional that he took his own life."

"You're twisted," said the cashier.

"Thank you," said Sarah R.

* * * * *

Sarah R. awoke the following afternoon on the couch in the cashier's apartment, her head throbbing from the margaritas they had drunk the night before. She went into the bathroom and looked at herself in the mirror. She noticed that her hair had begun to sprout.

The cashier wasn't home, but he did leave her an apple, a poppy seed bagel, and a note, which informed Sarah that he hadn't run away from her, that he had to work the morning shift at Café Hobbes, how she should feel guilty because she got to sleep off her hangover while he had to suffer through his to the sound of café blenders, that he thought she was the most beautiful bald girl he had ever seen, that she should know that his name was Jason Cooper, and that he should know what her name was since he would be waiting for her to return from L.A. He concluded the note with his phone number and address, and drew a blank line for her to fill in her name.

Sarah R.'s heart raced with joy, but joy was quickly replaced by the sobering thought of her ailing father almost a thousand miles away. She scribbled her name on the note and set off in the Nova to L.A. to find Zachary R.

115. On the Third Day

On the third day in the ICU, the nurse secured Zachary R. to the bed on which he had lain immobile since his rescue from the alley. She wheeled the whole apparatus into the hospital courtyard, which had grass of varying lengths.

The long blades were comic lifelines.

The medium blades were tragic lifelines.

The short blades were Hobbesian lifelines.

Drizzle beset Zachary R.'s face. He watched as best he could, a witness of renewal blinking in the pinprick rain.

Strapped down in the bed with only his head exposed, he thought, "I liked rivers and women."

Then he declared, "I am ready to die."

Suddenly Zachary R. stood up in what seemed to be the sky, except there were large double doors, like cellar doors, lit by the black sun of empathy. Zachary R. swung open the doors and returned to where he was in the years before his birth.

116. The Electric Light Dirge for Cello and Organ

After Zachary R.'s return to where he was in the years before his birth, the interested parties in Boston, Los Angeles, and New Orleans converged to arrange for the disposal of his earthly remains.

The hospital nurse from Los Angeles and the hot dog vendor were interviewed, along with asylum staff and various detectives from all three cities. Events were pieced together, and it was determined that Zachary R.'s body would be cremated and his ashes delivered to New Orleans, where they would be scattered in the exact middle of Lake Pontchartrain.

It seemed doubtful, at best, that either Zachary R. or Annabel R. would have wanted to be joined in death, let alone in a shallow, brackish lake at the mouth of the Mississippi that neither had visited during their lifetime. Nevertheless, this seemed to be the best option based on the available information.

Asylum staff in Boston suggested that the Electric Light Dirge for Cello and Organ be played at the funeral, which the hot dog vendor suggested take place in a small church near Café Macabre, because that was where Sarah R. was last seen.

It looked like Easter clouds and smelled like rain, like Annabel R., on the day of the funeral, which took place on the vernal equinox, the day Zachary R. had opened his backpack and showed Annabel R. the small poster ad for the carnival that had staked a patch of earth at the foot of the hill of shacks and cigarettes; the day when she wore the Revolution Dress and parted her hair down the middle; the day Zachary R. wore an indigo T-shirt and sideburns and his eyes blossomed like sunflowers; the day she led him to the photo booth by the fortune teller and sat him down and drew the curtain; the day they rode the parachutes, fired guns, and burned sage in the name of loneliness; the day it was so warm that the sky seemed to descend and nothing was distant; the day Zachary and Annabel moved through the carnival in such gentle oblivion that gypsy kids had no trouble stealing rolls of tickets from their pockets; the day Sarah R. was conceived.

The funeral was attended by the hot dog vendor and the hospital nurse from Los Angeles. Sarah R. did not attend. Despite a diligent search of most points between New Orleans, Boston, and L.A., she could not be found.

The hot dog vendor and the hospital nurse held hands as the Electric Light Dirge for Cello and Organ began to play, filling the small church and the air just outside the open windows and doors.

Then up came Bernrd Red in flannel pajamas that snagged his sores and made him grimace, and he heard the beautiful dirge out in the street and the music reminded him of a better time with Mozart and the nannies, and he stepped inside the small church and he joined hands with the hospital nurse and the hot dog vendor.

When the ceremony ended, the three of them hugged. The hospital nurse and the hot dog vendor told what they knew about the man whose ashes they held in an urn and were about to scatter across the lake.

"At least his wasn't a story about a boy and his dog," said Bernrd Red.

"Carry on, sir, madam," he said in his best concierge voice, and disappeared down the wet black street humming Crosby, Stills, Nash & Young, waxing reverent as stained glass at dawn.

After the hospital nurse did the honor of scattering Zachary R.'s ashes across the lake, she said to the hot dog vendor, "When some of the ashes blew back into my face, it was the same sensation as a feather boa."

117. A Nova Journey to L.A., Part 2

It was the evening before the vernal equinox when Sarah R. set off in the Nova to L.A. to find Zachary R., whose ashes would be scattered across Lake Pontchartrain the following morning. Sarah R. drove straight through the night and into the morning all the way to L.A., where she walked into a police station, identified herself, and explained to them about her father.

A detective at the police station made a brief investigation and discovered that her father was listed in the previous week's coroner reports.

"We've been looking for you," he said. "Please have a seat."

Sarah R. sat down in the chair that the detective pulled out for her.

"Your father passed away last week at Cedars-Sinai," said the detective, gently. "He had been living in an alley in Hollywood."

Sarah R. closed her eyes and silently repeated her Hobbesian mantra. The detective put his hand on her shoulder.

"Where is he now?" she asked.

"His body was cremated and the ashes were transported to New Orleans," replied the detective.

Sarah R. let out a staccato laugh of shocked disbelief. She sat in silence for several minutes.

"Can someone tell me where the alley is?" she asked.

"Yes," muttered the detective.

* * * * *

Sarah R. returned to the Nova and lay in the backseat, clutching the empty urn and alternating between crying and sleeping. She woke with the rising sun the following morning, bought sunflowers from an immigrant in a busy intersection, parked the Nova in Zachary R.'s stretch of pavement between medium buildings, placed the flowers in the empty urn, and set the arrangement down on the cleanest spot she could find.

Sarah R. stared at the sunflowers in the urn in the alley and found humanity at last. She headed off in the Nova back to Las Cruces.

EPILOGUE

The Goth Girls

When Zachary R.'s ashes were scattered across Lake Pontchartrain, the Goth Girls scattered throughout the twenty-first century, keeping the memory of Zachary R. close to their hearts, which are held within their Damien lockets.

The Goth Girls will gather again in the twenty-second century in the cathedrals, prisons, and streets of the world to select a troubled man to torment and to protect.

The Cold Angel

After the Cold Angel said goodbye to Zachary R. and disappeared into the fog, she had nothing but time to reflect on the outcome of her final mission in service to mankind. She thought about how she had led Zachary R. to his moment of clarity in the New Hampshire mountains, and about how little effect this ultimately had on his fate. She thought about what Zachary R. had said: "Sometimes the shivers are painful, but you make the shivers feel good." Then she recalled her own advice: "You have been lying to yourself for a long time, but you don't have to suffer anymore."

Now the Cold Angel understood that her final mission was as much in service to herself as it was for Zachary R. She thanked God for granting her the wisdom to understand, and then she asked Him to bless what she now knew to be her true calling.

The Cold Angel, complete with veil, hands like winter, and the power to summon and control the movement of fog, visits fever patients around the world and makes their shivers feel good.

The Cracked Snail

The Cracked Snail continues to slither among the blades of the asylum lawn, thinking "Service to mankind," eating poison pellets for the pain, and looking fondly at one of its portraits that Zachary R. drew, portrait number one hundred and forty-five, which had blown across the asylum lawn and lodged in the lavender bush.

The Cracked Snail will continue to talk to asylum patients in the searing mental sun until the asylum closes its gates forever.

Bernrd Red

Bernrd Red still lives passive and uneasy, cantankerous and celibate, in New Orleans. He wanders the streets of the French Quarter, singing "Carry on, love is coming to us all."

Acknowledgments

Special thanks to my editors, Laura A. Lionello and Greg Dalgleish, for their expert guidance in the evolution and completion of this book.

About the Author

Douglas Richardson was born on February 20, 1967, in Duluth, Minnesota, and was raised in Camarillo, California. He currently lives in Los Angeles, where he works as a proofreader, editor, novelist, and poet. This is his debut novel.

www.ingramcontent.com/pod-product-compliance
Lightning Source LLC
Chambersburg PA
CBHW070220260626
47160CB00002B/621